THE INVISIBILITY MACHINE

"My turn now," Danny said eagerly, when everything was ready.

He took his seat on the stool, and the Professor fitted the gauntlets on his hands and the helmet over his head. The machine was snapped on, and as Irene had done, Dan looked out through the lenses of the dragonfly.

Like Irene, he practiced handling the device, flying it about the laboratory and growing used to the controls. Then he sailed out of the window and swung over the lawn and around the side of the house. . . .

Danny Dunn Invisible Boy

Danny Dunn Invisible Boy

Jay Williams and
Raymond Abrashkin

Illustrated by Paul Sagsoorian

AN ARCHWAY PAPERBACK
POCKET BOOKS • NEW YORK

POCKET BOOKS, a Simon & Schuster division of
GULF & WESTERN CORPORATION
1230 Avenue of the Americas, New York, N.Y. 10020

Published by arrangement with McGraw-Hill, Inc.
Library of Congress Catalog Card Number: 73-17415

ISBN: 0-671-29984-0

First Pocket Books printing September, 1975

10   9   8   7   6

Trademarks registered in the United States and other countries.

Printed in the U.S.A.

Contents

Danny Dunn Invisible Boy

The Great Cookie Plot

Danny Dunn was busy with a fascinating scientific experiment in aerodynamics. With his mop of red hair bent low over his work, he was attempting to design a paper airplane.

He had an idea for one that would be an improvement over the old-fashioned, triangular type which everyone learns how to make almost as soon as they learn how to fold paper. He had drawn up the plans for a stubby-winged and long-bodied jet, had worked out the geometry of the various folds that would be necessary, and now, his brows drawn together in concentration, was following the pattern using pages torn from a notebook. The only difficulty was that he was trying to carry out the experiment without Mr. Rizzi, the English teacher, noticing him.

Mr. Rizzi was at the blackboard, explaining the sonnet form.

"Please turn to the Shakespearean example on page fifty-two," he said. " 'Shall I compare thee to a summer's day?' "

Joe Pearson, in his seat near the front of the class, looked longingly out of the open window at the clear June sky. He had long since read all the poetry in the book, had learned the forms, and had also tried writing his own sonnets. Now he doodled on a scrap of paper:

> Thy talk is like a day in late July—
> It's long and dry.

"As you see," Mr. Rizzi went on, "the rhyme scheme is a-b-a-b, c-d-c-d . . ." He wrote busily on the board, while Danny made another careful fold and then had to stop because Mr. Rizzi turned around to face the class for a moment. Dan himself enjoyed poetry but the trouble was that he enjoyed solving problems even more, and sometimes he became so absorbed in a project that everything else became unimportant.

"Now let's look at the next page and compare the Shakespearean sonnet with the form Spenser used," said Mr. Rizzi, returning to the blackboard. Dan made three more folds, and the plane was finished.

"Pretty good," he said to himself, with satisfaction. It had actually taken two separate pieces of paper to do the job; one for the nose and wings, the other for the body and tail. "I'll bet this is the first improvement on the paper airplane since the Wright brothers."

But it wasn't enough to admire it. An invention has to be tried out. Danny began considering how he could give the plane a short test flight without distracting Mr. Rizzi from the pleasures of his lecture.

His friend, Joe, was in the next row and about five seats ahead. If Dan could get his attention, he might be able to send the plane gliding along to Joe while Mr. Rizzi's back was turned. According to his calculations, this model should fly very straight and very fast.

He thought of several plans to get Joe to look at him, including falling on the floor, or mixing a batch of $CH_3C_6H_2(NO_2)_3$ (otherwise known as TNT) and exploding it, but since neither of these ideas seemed practical, he settled for passing along a note which said, "Turn around." When Joe turned, Dan showed him the plane and mouthed the words, "Catch it." Joe nodded.

With a flick of his wrist, Danny shot the plane toward his friend. But he had designed it better than he expected. To his horror, it rose on a high, steep path like a real jet taking off. At the top of its trajectory, it leveled off and then dove. It hit Mr. Rizzi on the back of the neck, just as he was quoting from a sonnet by Milton.

" 'They also serve who only stand and wait' —ow!" said he.

There was a ripple of laughter from the class. Mr. Rizzi picked up the plane between thumb and forefinger with an expression on his face as if he were holding a dead mouse by the tail.

"Well, well," he said. "Paper airplanes. Now I wonder who sneaked into this class from the kindergarten?"

Nobody said a word. Danny felt his cheeks grow hot.

Mr. Rizzi was about to drop the plane into the wastebasket. But just then Eddie Philips, with a grin, said, "Why don't you ask Danny Dunn?"

Eddie's nickname among some of his classmates was "Snitcher."

Mr. Rizzi raised his eyebrows, for ordinar-

ily Dan was one of his best pupils. Before he could say anything, Dan said, rather weakly, "It was an accident."

"A crash landing, you mean," Mr. Rizzi said.

"Well, I really wasn't playing with it. I was just curious because last night Professor Bullfinch had some ideas about the physics of the relationship of wing to tail—"

"Nevermind," Mr. Rizzi interrupted. "You can explain all that to Mrs. Trinkaus in Science. For the time being, do you mind *very* much leaving the airfield long enough to join us for a sonnet or two?"

With that, he went on with his talk, leaving Danny feeling thoroughly squashed.

After school, Danny relieved his feelings somewhat by stepping not-quite accidentally on Eddie's toes at the lockers. Joe Pearson and Irene Miller were waiting for him, and the three went out together and cut across the sports field to the pleasant tree-shaded length of Elm Street.

Danny's father had died long before, and his mother had taken the job of housekeeper to the famous scientist and inventor, Euclid Bullfinch. The Professor had formerly been the head of the science department of Midston

University, but some of his inventions had brought him enough money so that he could retire and work at his own research in a private laboratory attached to his house. He had formed a great attachment to Dan, treating him as if he were his own son, and the boy's knowledge of science was greater than that of most adults. It was matched only by that of his friend, Irene, but where Dan was interested in physics and engineering, Irene had finally made up her mind to become a biologist. As for Joe, he knew very little about science, but made up for it by a wide range of knowledge about literature, art, music, and especially, eating.

"That Snitcher!" said Danny. "He must have extra eyes, or a periscope, or something. He always sees every mistake or everything a little bit wrong that anybody else does."

"Maybe he knows the secret of being invisible," said Joe. "Then he could have left his seat and tiptoed over to watch you."

"That's a lovely idea, Joe." Irene giggled. "But not very practical. He'd have had to know ahead of time that Dan was making the plane. I think it was just a good guess."

"He might have been wrong," Joe protested.

"But he wasn't," said Danny gloomily. "He

made me feel like an idiot. The worst of it is, now I'll have to start all over again and make another plane. Anyway," he added more cheerfully, "now I know it works. The Professor will be interested."

"I wish there *was* a secret of invisibility," said Irene, "and that I knew it. It would be awfully useful for my science project."

Irene was doing a study of birds and in particular, since it was late spring, of their nesting habits.

"How's it coming?" Danny asked.

"I'm almost finished with my field notes," said Irene. "I'll have to start putting the whole thing together pretty soon, making the charts and displays. My father loaned me a spotting scope and a pair of binoculars so that I've been able to watch the birds pretty well. But you know, there are so many leaves that it's hard to see them in their nests. If I could get right up to them without being noticed—"

"Maybe we can ask Professor Bullfinch if he knows how it can be done," Dan said. "Visibility is because light bounces off things, you know. So maybe there's a way of getting light to go around things, instead, and then you wouldn't see them."

"There's another kind of invisibility," Joe put in.

8

The other two looked at him in surprise. "I read it in a story by G. K. Chesterton," said Joe. "It was a mystery story, about a man who was murdered in a house that nobody could get into without being seen. People were standing in front of the house when it happened, and they'd have noticed anybody who went in. Later, the detectives found footprints in the snow going up to the front door and out again, right past those people, but they hadn't seen anybody go in or out. The murderer was invisible."

"How'd he do it?" Danny said.

Joe chuckled. "He was the mailman."

"I don't get it."

"Easy. Don't you see? Who'd notice a mailman—the man who always goes in and out of an apartment house? You'd think of a murderer as a sinister stranger, and that's what you'd be looking for."

"You can't really call that invisibility," Danny objected.

"Sure you can," said Joe. "Let's try it."

"Try it? How? Deliver mail somewhere and see if they notice us?"

"Quit kidding," Joe said. "I'm talking about a serious subject—food. When I was at your house yesterday, your mother was baking some lemon-almond cookies, right?"

"They were good, too. We had some after dinner."

"Stop torturing me. Are there any left?"

"Sure. Lots."

"Okay, let's be invisible and get some."

"I still don't see how I can pretend to be a mailman. My mother knows the mailman—"

"Forget the mailman!" Joe cried. "Put him out of your head. I'm talking about *noticing* people. Now look, if you go in first and say hello, and then we come in, your mother will stop noticing you because she'll be looking at us. It'll be just as if you were invisible. I'll say something to her, and while I'm talking, you get a handful of cookies."

"Hm. Seems logical," said Danny. "All right, let's do it."

They hurried their steps and were soon passing Irene's house. The Professor's house was next door, separated from it by large old maples, lilacs, and wide lawns. The three ran across the grass to the kitchen door.

Through the screen door, they could hear Mrs. Dunn singing to herself inside. Dan went in first, as they had agreed.

"Hi, Mom. I'm home," he said

"Obviously," said Mrs. Dunn, dropping peeled potatoes into a pot. She was a comfortable-looking woman, with hair as red as her son's. "Why are Joe and Irene standing outside? Have they suddenly become shy?"

"No, ma'am. We're coming in," said Joe, flustered.

He and Irene entered the kitchen. Nervously, Joe began talking, saying anything that came into his head.

"We were standing outside because I thought maybe it wasn't you in the kitchen. I mean, we heard singing and I thought what a beautiful voice, it can't be Mrs. Dunn—er, I didn't mean it that way—it sounded like an opera star . . ."

Mrs. Dunn, wiping her hands on her apron, inspected him thoughtfully. Then, without turning, she said, "Dan! Leave those cookies alone."

"Huh?" said Danny, from the pantry.

"You heard me. The rest of them are for the Women's Club Bake Sale. Come out here."

Danny came back into the kitchen.

"My gosh!" he said. "It's not fair. How did you know?"

"It's a motherly trade secret," said Mrs. Dunn smugly. "You don't expect me to give it away, do you? Only next time, tell your

friends to look at me when they talk to me, and not at the pantry."

"Very clever," said Joe. "I suppose my mother knows the same kinds of secrets. Is that what you talk about at the Women's Club meetings?"

"Get along with you," said Mrs. Dunn. "If you'll stay out from underfoot, I just might possibly let you each have a cookie a little later."

"Hello, Professor," Irene said suddenly.

No one had heard him come into the room. He smiled at them from near the doorway, a round-faced, bald, untidy man in an old tweed jacket. Usually, there was a jolly expression on his face behind his owlish glasses, but just now his smile had an uneasy quality.

"Ah—uh—yes, hello there, Irene," he said.

"Did you want something, Professor?" asked Mrs. Dunn.

"No, no, not a thing. I won't disturb you. I was just going back from the laboratory. I mean, back to the pantry—er—the kitchen. I mean, I'll just go back to the laboratory."

He moved quickly to the door, with an odd sideways kind of gait as if he didn't want to turn his back. As he vanished into the hall, Dan stared at Joe and then, with a nod, turned his eyes to the floor. Joe followed his gaze.

Where the Professor had been standing, there were cookie crumbs.

2

A Happy Accident

"After him!" snapped Dan.

He darted out of the room with the other two at his heels, while Mrs. Dunn gaped after them in astonishment.

The hallway ran the length of the house, with the living room, dining room, and study opening off it. A flight of stairs, wide but steep, led up to the other floors. Alongside the stairs, the hall ran to what had once been the back door of the old house, but which now opened into the Professor's laboratory. This was a good-sized room, or rather pair of rooms since it had been partitioned off at one end to make a small office. Here the Professor kept his files and notes, a library of technical books, and a telephone hookup with the big computer at Midston University, which he was allowed to use. The other room, the lab proper, contained all sorts of special equipment which the Professor used in his researches.

The three friends burst into the room. Professor Bullfinch had just closed the door behind him, and was almost bowled over when it flew open again.

"What—?" he began.

Danny pointed at him dramatically. "Joe, Irene—do you see what I see?" he said.

"You mean Professor Bullfinch? Sure I see him," said Joe. "We just followed him in here, didn't we?"

"I don't mean that. Look at the front of his shirt."

There were more cookie crumbs on it, and the Professor made a futile effort to brush them off.

"I don't understand what all the fuss is about," he said mildly.

"We were trying to make Danny invisible, but it didn't work," said Irene. "And then you used the very same trick—while Mrs. Dunn was talking to us, she didn't notice you sneaking into the pantry. That's a terrible thing for a grown-up to do to three poor innocent children."

"Hungry children," put in Joe.

"I repent," said the Professor. "I'll pay a fine if you'll promise not to take the case to court."

He pulled out a handful of cookies and passed them around.

"What's all this about making Danny invisible?" he continued, biting delicately into one of the crisp morsels.

Danny explained their conversation, and the plan they had made.

"Do you think, Professor," he said, "it would be possible to make somebody really invisible?"

"By camouflage," said the Professor, taking out his pipe and filling it slowly. "If you wanted to be invisible in a forest, the best way would be to look like a tree. Another way is to be so visible that nobody notices you. As in Edgar Allan Poe's story 'The Purloined Letter'—"

"I read that," Joe said. "You mean, someone didn't want a letter to be found, so he left it right out in plain sight on the mantlepiece, and nobody saw it."

"That's not real invisibility," Danny protested. "Well, I suppose it is in a way, but it isn't what I mean. I mean, being able to walk around in a room full of people without being seen, for instance."

Professor Bullfinch struck a match, and stood looking at it with a slight frown until it burned his fingers.

"Drat the thing!" He dropped it, sucked a scorched finger, and struck another match. "I don't think so, Dan," he said, lighting his pipe. "The problem is in the nature of light. We see because light bounces off things and returns to our eyes."

"Yes, but if we could bend the light around a thing you wouldn't be able to see it."

"You know better than that, Dan. It takes a lot of gravity to bend light—the pull of an enormous star, for instance."

"But there are some materials that are naturally invisible," said Irene. "Glass, for instance. And crystals bend light, don't they? That's how a prism operates."

"Yes, some matter is transparent and lets a lot of light through, or bends the light away from itself to a certain extent. It isn't really invisible, though. Just think about it—look at those windows." He gestured with his pipe stem. "They refract—or bend—the light, and also reflect it. You can see them, can't you? You see the light shining on the glass and the reflection of things in this room. No," he went on, "the trouble is that we can't separate the optical properties of matter from its chemical properties. The ability to bend or absorb light is related to the atomic structure of matter. And the same is true of living things—you just can't change their chemical or atomic properties so that they become like a glass or crystal. We might make mechanisms which are hard to see, by making them out of matter with a high refractive index, but we couldn't do it to living things, like people."

Dan's face fell. He had already made up his mind that the Professor could solve the problem.

"Oh, well," said Irene. "It was fun thinking about it, anyway."

The Professor chuckled. "There is another way," he said. "You could do it by inventing a machine that would be the next best thing to invisibility."

"I don't get it," Danny said.

Irene shook her head. "Neither do I. What's the next best thing to being invisible, Professor?"

"What I'm thinking of," replied Professor Bullfinch, "is a tiny device full of sensors which would pick up the signals of light and touch and send them back to a receiving station. You've all seen spy stories on television in which a 'bug' is put somewhere in a room and sends back voice signals to a listener. If it's small enough, it isn't noticed. Well, if you could make sensors tiny enough, they could send back the images and the touch of things, as well as sounds. Then, if you had the right equipment to receive the information, it would be just as if you were standing invisibly in that room."

Joe sighed. "I don't think much of that idea."

"Don't you understand it?" said Danny. "It's perfectly clear."

"Sure, I understand it all right. But what's the good of it? You could see and smell and touch a beautiful dinner, but you couldn't eat it."

"Joe," said the Professor solemnly, "you're in danger of becoming a slave to your stomach."

"I don't mind that kind of slavery." Joe grinned.

"It sounds like a swell idea to me, Professor," said Danny. "What about making a machine like that?"

Professor Bullfinch shook his head. "Not just yet, Dan. We haven't the necessary materials to make switches and amplifiers small enough to be practical. Maybe some day—"

"I'm just as glad," muttered Joe. "I have a feeling it would only lead to trouble."

"Don't be so pessimistic." Irene laughed.

Dan, meanwhile, had been looking at one of the stone-topped laboratory benches at which the Professor had been working. Among a litter of papers and notebooks, electrical parts, and various pieces of equipment stood a tripod on which was a metal container. In it was a small quantity of what looked like coarse sugar.

"What's this stuff, Professor?" Danny asked. "Are you trying a cooking experiment?"

As he spoke, he dipped a finger into the container, intending to pick up a few grains and taste them. Professor Bullfinch caught his hand.

"Not so fast," he said.

Danny looked up at him. "Sorry. Is it poisonous?"

"I don't think so. But it's rather rare, and I can't spare any."

"What is it?" said Irene.

"Something my old friend, Dr. Grimes, sent me," said the Professor.

"How is Dr. Grimes? Is he still in Washington?" Joe said.

"Oh, yes, heading an important project for the Academy of Scientific Research. He's as sour as ever. When he sent me this stuff"— the Professor motioned to the metal container—"he wrote, 'You are far too dreamy to see the practical applications, but perhaps you will find a little time for studying the material between your nonsense games.'"

The Professor had imitated his old friend's stern voice so well that the children burst into laughter. "Good old Grimes," Professor Bullfinch added. "He gets as much pleasure out of being grumpy as most people do out of being cheerful."

"But what is the material?" asked Dan.

"It's something new they've developed which I think has good possibilities as a semiconductor," the Professor answered. "I have diffused a p-type impurity through the crystals, and when I pass an electrical current through one of them, I am hoping it will flow one way but not the other. That will, in effect, give me an off-on switch. As you know, such miniature switches are the basic elements of any computer."

Dan and Irene nodded. Joe said airily, "Oh, yes, I did know but I'd forgotten."

"Are you going to test the crystals now, Professor?" said Danny.

The scientist put his pipe into his pocket. "I had everything prepared," he said, "and only stopped for a little refreshment. The test itself is quite simple. I suppose it's no good my trying to get you all to leave me alone?"

They shook their heads.

"All right. Take a look at it, first."

He pointed to a large, gleaming, powerful microscope which stood on the lab table next to the metal container. Dan peered into the eyepiece. He saw what appeared to be a shining white brick with several thick wires leading from it. It was, in fact, only one tiny crystal and the wires were finer than strands of hair. They ran from the microscope to connect with another machine, on the face of which was a dial. Dan stepped back and let the others take their turns.

"Now, we'll see," said the Professor. "I'll try passing the current through it. The dial will register the amount of flow."

He snapped on a bright lamp that stood on the bench, so that he could see better.

There was a sharp *pop!*

It came from the electrical cord of the lamp, which trailed across the top of the lab table. A light puff of smoke rose among the

mass of papers, and then a little tongue of flame shot up.

"It's on fire!" Irene exclaimed.

Danny was already in action. In his usual headstrong way, he grabbed up the first thing that came to hand—a beaker full of clear liquid that stood on the bench.

"Wait! Stop!" yelled the Professor. "That's not—"

Dan had already dashed the liquid over the fire. At once, blue flames sprang up fiercely, surrounding both the metal container and the microscope.

"—water," finished the Professor, with a sigh.

He took two long strides and yanked the cord plug out of its wall socket. Meanwhile, Joe had snatched a heavy canvas apron from a hook and used it to smother the flames.

"Oh, gosh," Danny said ruefully. "I just didn't think. I should have remembered that you aren't supposed to try to put out an electrical fire with water, anyway."

"Quite right," said the Professor. "And that wasn't water—it was alcohol. I use it for cleaning junctions." He inspected the mess on the table, shaking his head. "You really must learn to count to ten before you act, Dan."

"What happened?" said Joe. "Did the experiment blow up?"

"Oh, no. It was a short circuit in the lamp wire. There was a worn spot in the insulation," Professor Bullfinch said. "When I turned on the lamp, that spot gave way, and the spark jumping the wires set the papers underneath on fire. Then when Dan threw the alcohol over it, that's what blazed up and—"

He stopped short. He was bending over the metal container, and he straightened with a stricken look. "Great heavens!" he said.

Danny's heart sank. "What's—what's the matter?"

Irene was already looking into the metal container. Where the sugary crystals had been there was a grayish blob.

"It's melted!" she blurted.

"Maybe it's really marshmallow," Joe mumbled.

Professor Bullfinch glanced into the eyepiece of the microscope. "This one has melted as well," he said. "Oh, dear. And that's all I have of the stuff. I shall have to write to Grimes and explain. Perhaps he'll send me some more. But he won't be very pleased."

Danny groaned. "Gosh, I'm *really* sorry."

"Don't take it too hard, my boy," Professor Bullfinch said, in his kindly way. "After all, you weren't responsible for the short circuit. That was my fault. I knew that wire was frayed, but I'd been putting off repairing it."

Danny felt a little better. "Maybe the stuff will still work," he said. "I mean, even if it's melted, maybe it'll still act as a semiconductor. Don't they have semiconductors which aren't crystals?"

Professor Bullfinch stood with his chin in his hand for a moment, staring at Danny. Then he said, "Some experiments have been tried with amorphous conductors, but so far without much success. Still . . ."

Decisively, he turned to the microscope. "The wires are still unharmed. The flames didn't last long enough to do them any real damage."

He checked over the rest of the electrical hookup. "Seems all right," he said. "Very well. Let's give it a try." He snapped a switch.

Danny pointed wordlessly to the dial. Its needle had swung all the way over.

The Professor made an adjustment or two, and touched another switch. At once, the needle dropped to zero.

"Amazing!" he breathed. "The stuff allows an enormous flow one way, and none at all the other."

"Do you mean that it works after all?" said Irene.

"Better than I ever expected," said the Professor. "But it will take some testing and experimenting. By George, this may mean—"

He swung around on the children. "Shoo!" he said. "I've got to get to work."

"But—" Danny began.

"No buts. It may work out that your accident has turned into a benefit," said the Professor. "Right now, however—out."

When the Professor spoke in that firm voice, there was no argument. In silence, the three filed out of the lab.

"I suppose he'll tell us sooner or later if it's successful," said Danny. "But I don't know how I'm going to wait."

29

3

"Is It?"

Nevertheless, he had to wait. The days passed and slowly turned to weeks.

Almost every day, at first, he would say to the Professor at breakfast or dinner, "Anything new?" And the Professor would smile silently, or say, "Don't be impatient, my boy." "But I can't help being impatient," Danny would say. "It's the way my head is made."

After a time, however, other things crowded in on him and Dan forgot about the new material and the Professor's experiments with it. There was schoolwork to do, a science project to prepare—Dan was building a model to demonstrate the way a radar beam operates—and at the end of June a big

Field Day to be held by the Midston Civic Club. There would be races and sports events, finishing up with a baseball game, and Danny hated to let a day go by without some batting practice.

The two teams were made up of the upper grades, and they were all practicing on the school diamond one morning during what was supposed to be the gym period. It was the last lazy week of school after exams, and everyone, including the teachers, was relaxed. There were no regular classes, but instead the periods were taken up with special events, exhibitions, and assemblies. It was, Joe said, the only time you could thoroughly enjoy school.

Mr. Baum, the gym teacher, was pitching. Danny had just finished smacking a long drive to center field, and Irene took the bat.

"I wouldn't play on a team with a girl on it," said Eddie Philips in a sneering voice.

"You'd better move back," Irene said politely. "You know how wildly we girls swing. I just might miss the ball and clobber you."

Eddie stepped hastily away. Mr. Baum threw a fast ball, and Irene swung at it. Snitcher had made her angry, however and she hit it at an angle. It looped up gracefully and landed behind her. Snitcher laughed raucously.

Irene tightened her lips. She sent the next ball sailing past the shortstop.

"Good hit!" called Mr. Baum. "Who's next?"

"Give me that bat," said Snitcher. "I'll show you how it's done."

He was as good as his word. He was a heavily built boy and he put his shoulders behind

the swing. The ball screamed out to the far end of the field.

"Pretty good," Danny said warmly. "That would have been a homer."

"You don't have to tell *me* what it would have been," said Snitcher, handing the bat carelessly to George Bessel, who was next. "You'll have to get some better players than girls on your team. My bunch is going to smear you."

Joe, who was lying on the grass with his hands behind his head, said, "You talk a great game, Snitcher. You don't really need any other players on your team."

"Very smart. I don't see you playing."

"I don't dare. I'm scared of you." Joe grinned. "Anyway, baseball is for the common people. We noblemen go in for tougher games."

"Oh, yeah, Miss Arnold's big spell," Snitcher jeered. "I'm going to win that, too."

Miss Arnold, one of the most popular teachers, was holding a spelling bee later in the week, with a small portable radio as the prize.

Joe yawned. "Good luck," he replied. "You'd better start learning some words with more than three letters in them, then."

Snitcher stalked away.

"You can laugh at him," Danny said, "but you know he really is pretty good at spelling."

"Sure, I know. But I'm better than he is, and he knows *that*," Joe said complacently.

The three friends walked home together after school, as they generally did. Irene said, "I'll have to go right home. I have to finish up my charts for the science exhibition tomorrow. I just have an hour's work and I want to get it done."

"My project's finished," Danny said. "So I'll help you."

"And I'll watch," said Joe. "There's something soothing about watching other people work."

They stopped at Dan's house long enough for him to tell his mother where he was going. Then they went next door and up to Irene's room. All the flat surfaces—the desk, table, bed, bureau—were covered with sheets of cardboard on which she had mounted photos and drawings of birds, or illustrated charts showing the nesting cycle of the Baltimore oriole from the building of the nest to the final flight of the young birds. There was also a branch set into a wooden stand with an oriole's nest hanging from it. Any free space was taken up by colored marking pens, paste, scissors, magazines, and reference books.

"The biggest problem about this project," said Joe, "is where do we sit down?"

Irene cleared some sheets of paper from a chair. "You can sit there," she said. "And since I know you're pretty good at lettering, you can start printing at the top of this sheet, *Third Week*."

Joe groaned. "I might have known it. Some people just can't stand to see a person enjoying himself."

They got to work, and for a time all was quiet. The delicious smell of the newly mowed lawn came to them through the open window, just outside of which hovered a dragonfly on glittering wings. Now and then a bird called.

At last, Danny said to Irene, "I've been thinking about what Snitcher said. Does it bother you much to be the only girl on the team?"

"Some," Irene admitted. "I get the feeling that everybody is looking twice as hard at me as at anyone else. They expect me to do worse than everybody else—or maybe better. Either way, it makes me nervous."

"You're not thinking of quitting, are you?"

"Certainly not."

"Good. Don't let it get you down."

Joe tipped his head back to admire his neat lettering. "You know, it's funny," he said.

"There'll be both boys and girls in the spelling bee, and nobody thinks anything about it. There'll be boys and girls with exhibits in the science show—if there were only boys, people would think it was peculiar. So why should they think it's so strange if there are boys and girls playing baseball together?"

"It's because girls aren't supposed to be good at games," said Irene.

"No, that's not it, because girls do play all the games boys do and everybody knows it."

"Well, boys are supposed to be better at them."

"Whoever made up that rule didn't know about me," Joe protested. "The only game I'm any good at is checkers."

"Or what about George Bessel?" said Danny. "He runs about as fast as an inchworm, and can't throw a ball any farther than across the street. The only reason he's on Snitcher's team is that they're friends."

They went on working and were just finishing up when Mrs. Miller called up the stairs, "Irene! Telephone!"

Irene ran off to answer it. She returned with a bewildered look.

"That was Professor Bullfinch," she said. "He wants us all to come to the lab right away." She hesitated, and then added, "And he said, 'Tell Joe I'm no good at games, either.' "

Joe's mouth dropped open. Danny said, "How did he know?"

"Let's go find out," said Irene.

They found the Professor seated on a high stool before one of the laboratory benches, writing busily in a notebook. He glanced up as they charged through the door opening to the back yard.

"Ah," he said, "the only girl on the team. I'm glad you're not thinking of quitting."

They gaped at him in astonishment. He went on, "I liked your lettering, Joe. In fact, Irene, the whole display looks very attractive."

"How did you—?" Danny stuttered. "Where were you—?"

"Right there in Irene's room with you." The Professor chuckled. "But I never left this spot."

He stood up and touched a curious-looking device which they now noticed on the bench beside him. It resembled a crash helmet, with a visor that projected to cover the whole face of the wearer. Next to it was a pair of clumsy gauntlets. Cables connected both helmet and gauntlets with a metal box, on the front of which was a kind of miniature piano keyboard and a couple of small knobs.

"This," he said impressively, "is an invisibility simulator with intromittent transmission."

There was a long moment of silence, and then Joe said, "A which what? I never heard of such a thing."

"Yes, you have," said Danny excitedly. "We all have. I know what it is. It's the thing you told us about a long time ago, right here in the lab, isn't it, Professor?"

Professor Bullfinch nodded. "I suggested, you remember, that something might be made that would be just as good as being invisible. But I told you we didn't have the right materials to make sensory devices, switches, or amplifiers small enough. Well, now we have —thanks to dunnite."

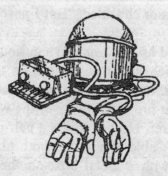

"Dunnite?"

"The stuff you produced by accident, when you melted Dr. Grimes's crystals. It is amazing—the best semiconductor I've ever tested. It allowed me to make ultra-microscopic transistors."

He reached across the helmet and picked up something small and glittering.

"A dragonfly!" said Irene.

"Not really," said the Professor. "It only looks like a dragonfly. It's the sensory probe."

He handed it over so they could inspect it. It was made of light, clear plastic, through which they could see that its insides were packed with the tiniest machinery imaginable. The wings were rigid, and covered with a design of very fine wires.

"I'll explain how it works," the Professor

39

continued. "The 'dragonfly' flies by jets of compressed air. Also, since it's so light in weight, it can operate like a glider, taking advantage of air currents. The wings are also antennae for receiving power, which is beamed to it by microwave.

"The 'dragonfly' can be flown to a particular spot. There, it picks up sensory data—images, sounds, and touch—and broadcasts them back by microwave to screens and receivers inside the helmet and gloves. So by sending it to Irene's windowsill, I was able to watch you and listen to you as if I were there myself."

Danny gave a long whistle. Then he burst out, "Can we—"

The Professor laughed. "—Try it? I knew you'd ask that. Yes, you can, my boy. You all can. But first I must give you some instruction in operating it. It's not easy."

"What was it you called it?" Joe said. "An invisibility—?"

"—simulator with intromittent transmission. In other words it imitates invisibility by sending back signals."

"Yes. Isit."

"Yes, it is," said the Professor, looking puzzled.

"No, I mean Isit is what it is."

"Is It?"

Professor Bullfinch blinked. "You're confusing me, Joe. It is what it is, isn't it?"

"Sure it is. It's Isit," said Joe. "Invisibility Simulator with Intromittent Transmission. I-S-I-T."

"Of course," said the Professor. "I see what you mean. A good name. I hereby christen it Isit." He shook his head. "I hope I can keep this straight in my own mind. Isit is *it*."

4

Irene's Flight

Professor Bullfinch pulled the high stool over so that it was in front of the machine. "Who is to go first?" he said.

"I think Danny should," said Irene. "You wouldn't have the thing at all if he hadn't thrown alcohol on the fire."

"That's no reason for going first," Danny retorted. "Even though it worked out all right, I acted like a dope. Why don't we just draw straws?"

"That's the fairest way," agreed the Professor.

He rummaged around on the table and found a wire cutter. From a piece of copper wire, he snipped three bits of different lengths.

"Shortest goes first," he said. He held them out between his fingers so that only the ends showed.

They all drew at the same time. Irene's was the shortest. Next came Dan, then Joe.

"I'm just as glad to be last," Joe said. "That way, I'll find out what *not* to do."

The Professor made Irene sit on the stool. He helped her pull the gauntlets over her hands.

"They'll feel awkward at first, but you'll get used to them," he said. "The general idea is easy enough. These levers move the wings so that you can make the dragonfly rise, dip, or turn in the air. Put your thumbs on the buttons in the knobs. Those control the air jets. Got that?"

Irene nodded.

"Now I'll put the helmet on you. I'll switch on the sensors myself, at the keyboard. Take a minute and get ready."

Inside the helmet, all was dark. Irene felt an instant of panic, as if she were shut up in a closet. She had difficulty breathing and little golden dots swirled before her eyes.

"I'm pressing the keys," said the Professor. "Don't be frightened. Everything will seem rather strange."

It was more than strange. She seemed to be looking across a great gray space with a jumble of mountainous shapes rising on either

side. Although she could still feel the control levers in her hands, she also seemed to be touching something hard and flat.

"I don't know where I am!" she said.

"Take it easy," the Professor said soothingly. "You are looking at four curved screens inside the helmet, and seeing through the lenses of the dragonfly's eyes. It's lying on the lab bench, so you may feel a little mixed up at first."

As he spoke, Irene began to sort out what she was seeing. She could make out, now, that the gray was the stone surface of the worktable, and that the shapes around her were notebooks and pieces of apparatus. The control box for Isit towered up beside her.

"Now, then," the Professor went on, "the dragonfly also has a set of hooks, or claws, under its body. You can use these to have it cling to things or even to pick up small objects. Squeeze your hands around the knobs and that will make the claws close. Try it.'"

Irene did so and felt as if her fingernails were scraping along the hard surface.

"Very good. I saw them move," said the Professor. "Now you're ready to try a flight. The right hand controls the forward jet, the left the backward one. Does the way look clear?"

"Yes."

"Give it a forward burst, then—very gently! Not too much! Remember, the dragonfly weighs only a few ounces."

Gingerly, she pressed her right thumb down for a moment. She felt herself glide forward and saw the edge of the table shoot toward her. The next instant, she was in the air.

Everything was very real, so that she forgot she was merely looking into screens inside the helmet, or hearing sounds through amplifiers, or experiencing the touch of things through sensory devices. She seemed to be actually soaring, and she could even feel the rush of the air past her body. The far wall of the laboratory loomed closer and closer, and in sudden fright she pulled back one of the levers, forgetting which was which.

She felt herself leaning to the right, and skimmed away from the wall. She had a wild image of windows shooting past, and a glimpse of Joe, open-mouthed, below her. The Professor was shouting something, which at first she was too scared to understand. Then she made herself calm down.

"Touch the backward jet—the left one," he was saying. "It will slow you down."

She remembered, then, and pressed her left thumb down just for a second, and felt her movement slowing. She could feel an upward push of air, and as she slid into it, it lifted her lightly. Balancing as if she were on a tight-rope, she let the air carry her on a wide spiral path toward the ceiling.

Now she was getting the knack of it. She found she could sense the different layers of air, some lighter and warmer, some heavier and colder, and feel the movement of their currents. She began to enjoy herself. It was like one of those wonderful dreams of flying. She turned easily in a half-circle, and glancing down, saw that she was above the Professor and the two boys. They were staring up with strained faces.

She saw something else—something that made the whole thing even more dreamlike. She saw *herself*, sitting on the stool next to the Professor, her head covered by the closed helmet, her hands inside the gauntlets, grasping the levers on the box.

It was so eerie to look down at herself this way that she almost lost control of the dragon-fly, and only when she felt herself beginning to wobble in the air did she set herself, tight-lipped with concentration, back to flying.

"I'm okay," she called, forgetting again that she was not really above them but right beside them.

She gave herself a little boost with the forward jet and slipped sideways and forward out of the warm upward current. On a long, even glide she skimmed right out of one of the windows and into the open air.

"Don't take the dragonfly too far," the Professor said warningly. His voice seemed to come from the empty air next to her. "The microwave beam has a limited range."

She scarcely heard him, since she was so absorbed in seeing the lawn, the flowerbeds, and the trees from a position about twelve feet above the ground. Using her forward jet again, she sailed toward a row of thick bushes. The leaves came toward her swiftly, and just in time she slowed herself with the backward jet and landed on a twig. She felt its smooth bark under her hands and squeezed both fists so that the claws of the dragonfly closed around the twig and held her in place.

Leaves were all about her, and she could see little except their jagged edges and their glossy surfaces. She could count the tiny hairs on their undersides. One difficulty, she now found, was that she couldn't turn her head—or rather, the dragonfly's head. Its bulging lenses gave her a wide field of view, something like looking out of a curved window, but to see beyond that range meant that she would have to turn the whole body of the machine, which was something she didn't know how to do.

The branches around her suddenly dipped, and she was bounced sharply as if she were on a springy couch and someone else had jumped on it. There was a flutter nearby, and she realized that a bird had landed on the bush. It must be behind her somewhere, just out of sight.

"How do I turn this thing around?" she said aloud.

"Where are you—it, I mean?" said the Professor.

"I'm in a bush on the edge of the lawn. There's a bird here somewhere, and I want to look at it."

"You can't turn while you're perched. You'll have to take off, turn in the air, and land again."

"Okay. Oh—can the bird hear me talking?"

"Of course not, Irene. You're not out there —you're here!"

She felt the Professor tap her shoulder. "I keep forgetting." She grinned.

She opened the claws and shot out of the bush. She banked and turned, more confidently this time, and as she glided back to the bush, she saw a brown-and-white blur flash past her. Slowing herself, she now noticed a nest among the branches, and she was able to land just to one side of it and facing it.

Irene had spent many hours watching birds through her father's high-powered binoculars. But never before had she had such a clear, close view of a nest with babies in·it. She saw how skillfully it was woven together of thin twigs, bits of vine, and long grass stems to form a snug, deep bowl in which lurked three nestlings. They were snuggled close together, and she could see every damp-looking quill of their sprouting feathers.

"Robin or thrush," she said to herself.

With the thought, a shadow fell over her, and a wood thrush landed on the edge of the nest. He was so near that she could feel the wind of his arrival and could clearly see the way he dropped his tail to stall, raising his body and cupping his wings to make a neat landing. He paid no attention to her at all and with a thrill she told herself, "Professor Bullfinch was right. It's the same as being invisible!"

As the bird landed and the nest bounced, the young ones raised their heads. They opened enormous mouths, which looked much too big for their·skinny necks. Irene could look right down their red throats, just as the parent thrush was doing.

She was no more than six inches away and she stared at him in fascination. From her perch, he looked enormous. She could see the smudged, dark, arrowhead markings on his white front, his sleek reddish-brown back, and his bright black, intelligent eye. She could even see the tiny pulse throbbing in his breast, and she remembered that birds have a very high temperature and that their hearts beat as fast as ten times a second.

The thrush held a pale green caterpillar in his beak, and as she watched, he bent forward, thrust his beak far down into one of the gaping baby mouths and crammed it with food.

She watched for a moment or two longer, and then, when the thrush had finished and had flown off to look for more food, she decided to move on also. She was facing inward, so she gave a burst from the backward jet and whizzed into the open. It was not as easy to go backward as she had thought, and she found herself falling. The lawn spun up at her, and involuntarily she closed her eyes and gave a little scream. The dragonfly was too light to be harmed, however, and she felt only the soft rustle of grass as it touched the ground.

"What's the matter?" asked the Professor. "I'm on the ground. Now what?"

She heard the noise of running feet and then Danny's voice shouting, "I see her. I mean it. A little shiny thing out there in the middle of the lawn."

The Professor said, "Now, Irene, make sure you're level. Then give yourself a good boost with the jet and slowly pull back both control levers just a little, so that the leading edges of the wings catch the air—"

"Oh—right! I know. Okay."

She was doing it as she spoke, and she found herself rushing along the tips of the grasses. Then, abruptly, she was in the air, swooping steeply, higher and higher, until she was above the tops of the tallest trees.

She heard Danny yell, "Watch it!" At the same time, she saw a swallow diving straight at her out of the blue.

She was too startled to move. She saw the sharp, stubby beak open as the bird flicked its wings to turn in mid-air. Then it was upon her. She felt a blow that rocked her as the bird snapped its beak on what it thought was a tasty dragonfly.

The sky whirled about her. Then everything went dark and silent.

"Where am I?" she cried. "Am I eaten?"

Professor Bullfinch had shut off the machine and was lifting the helmet off her head.

Danny, at the window, said, "I see where it fell. It's in that big old maple."

"That's going to be some climb," Joe said. "We'll have to have a ladder to get into the lower branches."

"I still don't understand what happened," Irene stammered. "That swallow got me, didn't it?"

"It got the dragonfly," said Danny. "I saw it—did you hear me yell to warn you? Then the minute it found out the thing was plastic instead of a real insect, it dropped it. You fell —I mean It fell—into that tree."

"The bird must have damaged one of the wings or broken a connection," said the Professor. "You lost power when you lost contact with the beam. We'll fix it, though, as soon as somebody climbs that maple and gets the dragonfly back."

Danny and Joe were staring at Irene.

"We'll go right away," said Danny. "But— what was it like, Irene?"

She drew a long breath and let it out in a sigh.

"I don't know the right words," she said. "It was wonderful!"

5

Invisible Danny

The dragonfly was soon recovered from a fork high in the tree, and the Professor inspected it under the microscope.

"Not serious," he said cheerfully. "A broken connection, that's all. Our dragonfly isn't as fragile as it looks. This plastic is very tough, and even the delicate wings can take a lot of punishment. Almost the only thing we have to be afraid of is fire. It burns easily. When you are flying it, stay away from open flames or high-tension cables."

As he talked, the Professor had slipped his arms into metal sleeves on each side of the microscope. Moving his hands inside the sleeves, he could control very small, fine mechanical "hands" with which he was able to

work on the dragonfly under the microscope.
The repair was quickly made.

"My turn now," Danny said eagerly, when
everything was ready.

He took his seat on the stool, and the Professor fitted the gauntlets on his hands and
the helmet over his head. The machine was
snapped on, and as Irene had done, Dan
looked out through the lenses of the dragonfly.

Like Irene, he practiced handling the device, flying it about the laboratory and growing used to the controls. Then he sailed out
of the window and swung over the lawn and
around the side of the house. As he did so, his

mother emerged from the kitchen door and started up Elm Street. Danny followed her.

It was very odd, seeing his mother from just above her head rather than below it. She strode along, humming to herself, with not the slightest idea that her son was watching her and listening to her from a distance of a foot or so. Danny snickered to himself.

A neighbor came out of a side street and waved to her. Mrs. Dunn waited until the other woman had caught up with her, and they walked on together.

"Are you going to Freddie's?" the neighbor asked. Freddie was the grocer a few blocks away.

"Yes," said Mrs. Dunn. "I'm making a special dessert tonight—you know that marvelous recipe Angie does, lemon whipped-cream pudding? I suddenly discovered I haven't a lemon in the house."

"What's the occasion? Somebody's birthday?"

"Oh, no. I just like to see their faces when I put something new and unexpected in front of them. The Professor has as much of a sweet tooth as Danny, and they both love surprises."

"It's not a surprise anymore," Danny mumbled. He began to wish he hadn't followed his mother after all.

By then, they had come to the corner of Maple Street, and Dan pressed his thumb hard on the forward jet button and veered away.

"Where are you now, Dan?" said the Professor.

Just as in Irene's case, Dan was startled, since the voice seemed to come from the air beside him. The illusion of being over the street was so real that he had forgotten he was actually seated in the laboratory.

"I'm just going along Maple Street. There's Eddie Philips' house."

"All right. So far the beam has plenty of strength. I'll warn you if you seem to be getting too far away."

Dan was about to turn the dragonfly, when Snitcher came out of his house. Glancing about him furtively, he set off running.

"Where is he going in such a hurry?" Danny wondered, automatically turning the dragonfly to follow.

Snitcher ran northward a block to Washington Avenue. It was a wide street, and on the other side of it lay the school grounds. Snitcher paused, waited for the traffic light, and then darted across and made for the main building.

"Funny," said Dan. "Going back to school

at this hour? There's nobody there but the janitor."

With that thought, he continued his pursuit.

Snitcher went around to the rear of the building where a door stood open. He marched boldly in, with Dan gliding unseen a little way above and behind him. The door led to a corridor off which were storerooms, the furnace room, and the utility room.

"Mr. Hagen," Snitcher called.

The janitor, a beefy, gray-haired man, stuck his head out of one of the doors.

"What you want?" he growled.

"Mr. Hagen, I've got to go to my home room," Snitcher said, putting on a piteous look. "I left my pen there."

"Get it tomorrow. Not allowed after school hours."

"But it's my mother's pen," Snitcher whimpered. "It's her good silver ball-point. She loaned it to me for school today, and I left it in my desk. *Please,* Mr. Hagen. She'll— she'll murder me! I just remembered it. It'll only take a minute."

The janitor grunted. "Okay, then. But you come right out, hear?"

"Sure. Gee, thanks, Mr. Hagen. Just one minute, honest."

Danny had to admire it, it was a masterly

performance. There were even tears in Snitcher's eyes. Keeping close to the ceiling where he couldn't be noticed, Danny followed the other boy into the main corridor and along to the door of Miss Arnold's room. With a quick burst of his jet, he managed to slip into the room before the door swung shut. He sailed noiselessly to one of the windowsills and was able to turn as he landed so that he was facing the room and could see what was happening.

Snitcher went to his desk and fished out a silver pen. Then he hurried to Miss Arnold's desk. He pulled open the top drawer, took out some papers held together with a clip, and spread them out on the desk.

Dan flew over and circled slowly above him. He saw that the papers held lists of words. Snitcher was running his pen swiftly down the lists, and now and then he would jot a word on a pad.

"It's the spelling bee!" Dan exclaimed. "Hey! Cut that out!"

The other boy, of course, heard nothing. Danny was filled with indignation. Completely forgetting where he was, he let go the controls and tried to grab Snitcher.

The dragonfly at once wobbled, stalled, and dove to the floor.

"Ooops!" said Danny. He shook his head to clear it of dizziness.

"What is it? What's the matter?" the Professor said.

"I forgot to—" Danny began.

At the same moment, Snitcher, whose eye had been caught by the movement as the bug fell, said, "What's that?"

From the floor, Danny saw him straighten up, looking like a giant.

"A dragonfly?" Snitcher said. "How'd it get in here?"

Danny groped frantically for the controls. All he could think of was Snitcher picking up the dragonfly, examining it, and finding out that it was a tiny machine. He found the levers after a moment. However, Snitcher was paying no further attention to the bug but had bent over his work once more. Time was pressing, after all; at any moment, Mr. Hagen might come to see what was taking him so long.

"How do you get this thing in the air again?" fumed Danny.

"Take it easy," said the Professor. "I don't know where you are or what's happening, but don't get so excited."

"But he's going to finish in a minute and go," said Danny. "And then I'll be locked in this classroom."

Even as he was talking, Snitcher, having jotted down all the words he was uncertain of, had stuffed his pad into his pocket, scooped up the papers and put them back in the desk, and was walking toward the door.

Danny pressed down the forward jet button and yanked back both control levers. The dragonfly shot up at a steep angle. Dan saw the doorway hurtling toward him and held his breath. Just in time, Snitcher opened the door and Dan sped through it, clearing the top by an inch or two. At once, still at high speed, he banked to the right, and was just able to level off before hitting the opposite wall. He whizzed down the corridor for a moment before he remembered to slow himself with a couple of reverse jets. Then he swung back and followed Snitcher out of the building.

He flew the dragonfly home again without incident, back in through the window, and made a neat landing on the lab bench.

"Whew!" he said. "Get me out of here."

The Professor helped him out of the helmet and gauntlets.

"What on earth happened, my boy?" he said.

Danny looked from his face to those of Irene and Joe. "That cheater!" he said. "I saw him!"

"Who? What?" said Joe.

"What classroom were you talking about?" Irene asked.

"Ours." said Danny. He drew a long breath, and then told them what he had seen.

"Snitcher must have planned the whole thing yesterday," he finished. "I remember Miss Arnold putting the lists of spelling words in her desk, after she told us about the contest. He must have borrowed his mother's pen this morning and then purposely left it in his desk so that he could go back and get it. That's why he said that he was going to win the spelling bee, earlier today."

"It's awful!" Irene said. "We ought to do something."

"Right," Dan agreed. "I ought to go to Miss Arnold and tell her."

"Tell her what?" said Joe. "That you were invisible?"

"No, of course not. But I could tell her I saw Eddie go to the school and that I followed him and saw him copy some of the words . . ."

His voice trailed away.

"Well?" said the Professor, who was looking intently at him.

"Well, I can't," said Danny. "I wouldn't be any different from Snitcher, if I did. They'd have to call *me* Snitcher."

Professor Bullfinch smiled.

"But it's not fair," Irene protested. "Suppose he wins the spelling bee? He shouldn't be allowed to."

"Okay," said Danny. "Then you tell Miss Arnold."

There was a long silence. Irene's face grew red.

Danny turned to Joe. "What about you?"

Joe shook his head. "If he wants to win so badly that he's willing to cheat, that's his business. Maybe I'll beat him anyway." He sighed. "Well, maybe it'll be a tie," he said.

"We're stuck," Irene said gloomily. "Maybe the voice of his conscience will tell him to confess. Aside from that, I can't think of anything."

"Let's forget about him," said Joe firmly. "Who cares? I want my turn with Isit, now."

He sat on the stool and put his hands into the gauntlets, while the Professor put the helmet on him. Danny watched, as the dragonfly on the workbench moved a few inches and then took off like a miniature airplane. He knew what Joe was feeling and seeing, and he grinned as the dragonfly wavered in the air, regained its balance, and at last soared to and fro. It flew out of the window, and he went to stand with Irene and watch as Joe explored the garden and then flew the bug out of sight between the trees.

He could hear Joe muttering to himself inside the helmet, and he wondered idly where the dragonfly was now, but his mind wasn't really on it. Instead, he was thinking of what Irene had said.

"The voice of his conscience," he repeated to himself.

Fifteen minutes later, the dragonfly reappeared. It seemed to fly more heavily than before, dipping in the air and recovering itself. It glided into the laboratory and landed with the smallest of thumps.

Joe's voice was muffled by the helmet. "Don't touch it. It's sticky."

"Sticky?" said the Professor in surprise. He bent over and inspected it. "So it is. What have you done to it?" He lifted off the helmet.

"It's honey." Joe giggled. "I'm sorry. It was an experiment. I followed some bees and found a hollow tree where they'd made a hive. It was so interesting watching them at close quarters and not having to be afraid of being stung. Then I got to looking at all that honeycomb and I started wondering whether you could get any taste of it at all. You know, you can feel things through the machine. Well, I wondered whether you could taste them, too. That," he added, looking smugly at the Professor, "is what we call the scientific method. Isn't it?"

"Not exactly, Joe, but I approve of your curiosity. So you tried to pick up some honey and taste it?"

"And I got stuck in it. I couldn't taste it, but I could sure feel it. I thought for a minute I'd never get free. But at last I gave a good backward boost and broke loose. It made the bug heavier in the air and harder to fly."

"Don't worry about it," said the Professor. "I'll clean it off. I want to make a few adjustments, anyway."

He surveyed the three with a benevolent twinkle in his eyes. "Now that you've had your chances at invisibility—or near invisibility—are you satisfied?"

"It was very exciting," Irene said. The boys nodded in agreement.

"What are you going to do with it now?" asked Joe.

"I have to notify Dr. Grimes of my success. He'll be pleased, although he won't show it," said the Professor.

Irene glanced at the clock on the wall. "It's late," she said. "I've got to go. Good-bye, Professor, and thanks so much for letting me try Isit."

"Me, too," said Joe. "See you tomorrow, Dan."

They ran off. Danny rested his elbows on the lab bench and put his chin in his hands.

"I want to ask you something, Professor," he said. "I want to know if you can make one small change in Isit."

"That depends, Dan. What sort of change?"

Danny grinned. "I want to know if you can make it into the voice of conscience. I'll tell you my plan . . ."

6

An Interrupted Ball Game

Everyone in Midston watched the sky anxiously Saturday night, and listened nervously to the weather reports. But Sunday morning came with a golden sunrise, a clear sky, and the most refreshing of breezes. The members of the Civic Club who had planned the Field Day looked at each other with relief as they set up the day's events.

In the morning there were races of all sorts, including a wheelbarrow race for fathers and a baby race. There was an archery demonstration by the Midston Bowmen, who shot at ping-pong balls, broke balloons, and split arrows in the style of Robin Hood. There was a bed-making contest, a tug of war, and a fire-making contest with flint and steel by the Boy Scout Troop.

There was only one casualty. In the hundred-yard dash, Danny Dunn slipped and fell, twisting his ankle. He hobbled to the finish line and sat down, grimacing with pain.

"That puts me out of the ball game," he said ruefully. "I'll have to cheer you all on from the sidelines."

At noon, the refreshment stands were opened, and the smell of charcoal-broiled hot dogs and hamburgers filled the air. The littlest children ran shrieking with excitement, getting between everyone's legs. Families sat on the grass together and shared homemade pies and cakes.

At two o'clock, everyone got ready for the baseball game.

Snitcher was swaggering. He had won the sack race and, with Lenny March, the three-legged race as well. And three days before, on Thursday, he had won Miss Arnold's spelling bee and couldn't stop boasting about it. In spite of his cheating, it had been a hard struggle between him and Joe, for Joe had kept up with him for fifteen words after everyone else had dropped by the wayside.

"Hey, Joe," he kept saying now, "how do you spell 'inconceivable'?" Or, "Do you want to listen to my new portable radio? Some prize, eh?"

But Joe only grinned lazily at him, which took all the pleasure out of his taunts.

The two team captains, Snitcher and Patrick Conran, tossed up, and Pat's team went to bat first. During the first inning, Danny got up quietly from a place he had chosen at the back of the crowd. If anyone had been looking at him, they might have been surprised to see how rapidly his twisted ankle had healed, for he showed no trace of pain, but everyone's attention was fixed on the game. He winked at his mother, who nodded to him. Professor Bullfinch got up as well and together he and Dan hurried to the road, got into the car, and drove off.

By the end of the sixth inning, the score stood at four to two in favor of Snitcher's team. The seventh opened with Pat Conran being deliberately walked by Snitcher, who pitched every ball wide, since Pat was a dangerous batter. Jon Karrell, who batted next, was put out, but before that happened Pat had succeeded in stealing second base.

Then Joe came up to bat.

They had persuaded him to substitute for Danny, and had put him out in left field, where he spent most of his time composing a poem about sports. It began:

> Tennis makes an awful racket,
> Golf is like strong tee;
> Football has too many feet,
> None of them's for me.

As a result, he had missed an easy fly, making everyone groan. His first time up, he had been caught out on a foul tip. Now, he stood swinging the bat and sighing, looking uneasily at Snitcher who was winding up. The pitch came. He gulped, shut his eyes, and swung wildly.

There was a loud crack. The ball went soaring up, up, up, as if it never intended to come down again.

"Run!" yelled everyone.

Joe, in astonishment, started for first base, while Pat Conran sped toward third. Snitcher rushed from the mound to get under the ball, but unfortunately for him, so did the catcher.

They met in the middle underneath it. Snitcher fell one way, and the catcher the other. The ball rolled gently away.

Joe found himself on first base, while Pat raced home.

"Great work, Joe!" his teammates shouted.

"Nothing to it," said Joe, trying to sound casual.

Irene walked to the plate and picked up the bat.

Her first time up, she had singled. It had gone for nothing when Billy Carver had been put out. But as she was walking in to get her mitt, she overheard a man sitting on the grass say, "They ought to send her back to cooking class. Next thing you know, they'll try putting girls in the Little League."

The words had stuck with her and made her more nervous than angry. They were with her now, as she stood waiting at the plate. She hadn't fully realized that there would be grown-ups watching who felt that strongly about her playing.

As a result, she froze. Snitcher sent the first ball down, and Irene found she simply couldn't move. She stood with her bat ready, but all she could do was flinch as the ball passed her. The umpire called a strike.

"I've got to swing!" Irene told herself. "Even if I miss, *I've got to swing!*"

But she couldn't. A second strike was called. A man's voice shouted jeeringly from the sidelines, "Give her a rolling pin—that'll make her more comfortable."

That did it. Snitcher sent another straight,

fast pitch down, and Irene lashed out at it with all her might. The ball went whistling out to center field.

The fielder dove for it and scooped it up. And fumbled it.

"Butterfingers!" roared Snitcher.

Joe's long legs took him to third. Irene touched first and started for second.

"Keep going! Keep going!" yelled Pat Conran.

The fielder finally got the ball. By this time, everyone was shouting directions and calling for the ball to be thrown here or there. In confusion, the fielder hurled it wildly somewhere between first and second base, and during the scramble, Irene rounded third and

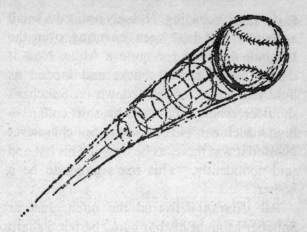

started for home. Joe was already there, being slapped on the back by everybody on the team.

The ball finally got to third—too late. The third baseman threw it home, but Irene had launched herself at the plate in a long, low slide.

"Safe!" cried the umpire.

Pat pulled Irene to her feet and hugged her. So did everyone else who could reach her. "Pretty good, Sis," called the man on the sidelines. Irene turned her back on him.

The score was now five to four in favor of Pat's team, and there it stayed until Snitcher's team was up.

The bases were loaded as Snitcher stepped

to the plate, scowling. Nobody noticed a small dragonfly that had been hovering over the baseball diamond for quite a while. Now it darted away, circled back, and landed as lightly as a puff of thistledown on Snitcher's shoulder, where it clung to his shirt collar behind his left ear. No one saw it. Snitcher never guessed it was there, as he waggled his bat and said confidently, "This one's going to be a homer."

Pat Conran delivered the pitch. Just as Snitcher brought his bat back, he felt a sharp pinch on his shoulder. He jumped, swung too late, and missed.

He looked around angrily, saying, "Who did that?" No one was close to him. He stared suspiciously at Bill Carver, who was catching, but it was obvious that Bill couldn't have done it.

The next pitch was high and wide. Then came a beautiful slow ball. It looked as though it couldn't be missed. Snitcher pulled back his bat, and at that very moment a tiny voice said in his ear, "Hey, Eddie!"

He gave a violent start, almost dropping the bat. The ball sailed majestically over the plate for a second strike.

Snitcher glared about him. "Who's doing

that?" he yelled. "Somebody's talking in my ear. Somebody pinched me. Who did it?"

The umpire said, "I've been watching, Eddie. Nobody's been anywhere near you. Come on, stop stalling. Play ball."

Pat glanced at the full bases, and scuffed his feet on the mound, getting ready for another pitch.

The tiny voice that no one but Snitcher could hear, said, "You're a cheat. You know it."

"I am not!" cried Snitcher.

"Cut that out," said the umpire. "You're trying to rattle the pitcher."

"I—I—" Snitcher stammered.

The little voice went right on. "How do you spell 'inconceivable,' Eddie?"

Snitcher shook his head in a maddened way, like a horse trying to shake off flies. Pat sent down a fast ball, but it was a good two feet away from the plate.

"Hit it!" said the little voice sharply.

Unable to stop himself, Snitcher swung.

"Strike three," called the umpire. "You're out."

Snitcher threw his bat on the ground. "Where are you?" he screeched. "Stop it!"

"I won't stop," said the voice. "I'm your conscience talking. I won't leave you alone until you confess that you cheated in the spelling bee."

Snitcher flailed around with both fists.

"It's no good trying to hit me," said the voice. "Tell the truth, Eddie Philips. You cheated."

"Help!" Snitcher howled. He began to run, stumbling blindly, and still the tiny voice went on relentlessly speaking into his ear.

Everyone had been watching Snitcher in alarm and amazement. Now, his father stepped forward and grabbed him by the arm. As he did so, the dragonfly detached itself from Snitcher's collar and flew off. Nobody paid any attention to it. It perched on the branch of a birch tree not far off.

"Now, what's this all about?" Mr. Philips said crossly.

"I'll tell, I'll tell," Snitcher babbled. "I sneaked into the school and copied the hard words. I cheated in the spelling bee! I'm sorry—I'm sorry— I'll give the radio back. Just tell it to shut up."

Mr. Philips looked grimly at his son. He was a very large man with a handsome, hard face and cold, blue eyes. Snitcher fell silent.

"I don't know what you mean by 'shut up,'" said Mr. Philips, "but if you cheated

in that spelling bee, we'll have a little talk about it. Who was second?"

"J-J-J——" said Snitcher.

"Me," Joe said modestly. "But I really don't want that radio. I'm just glad Sni— Eddie's conscience woke up."

"If he cheated," said Mr. Philips, in a voice with which there was no arguing, "then you won. You'll take the radio whether you want

77

it or not. Come on, Eddie. I apologize to the rest of you for breaking up the game."

"Oh, well, it was practically over anyway," said Pat.

Mr. Philips marched off, dragging his son with him.

If anyone had happened to be standing under the lowest branch of a nearby birch tree, they would have had the unbelievable experience of hearing a dragonfly laughing.

7

"Admit No One to This Laboratory!"

"It certainly went just as you hoped it would," said Mrs. Dunn.

They were discussing the matter at breakfast, the next morning. They had let her into the secret of Isit before the Field Day and told her of their plans, so that she wouldn't worry when Dan pretended to sprain his ankle, or be surprised when he and the Professor left the field.

"I couldn't believe that the Philips boy would do such a thing, when you first told me about it," she went on, dishing out eggs and bacon.

"There's a little wickedness in the best of us," said the Professor gently.

"Hmph! Speak for yourself," said Mrs. Dunn, pouring his coffee.

"You ought to try Isit, Mom," Danny said, with his mouth full. "It's great! Would you let her do it, Professor?"

Professor Bullfinch nodded. "If she likes."

"We'll see," said Mrs. Dunn. "It would certainly be useful for keeping an eye on you to make sure you did your homework."

"Oh," said Danny, in dismay. "Would you really? I never thought of that."

"It's just as I said," murmured the Professor. "There's a little wickedness in the best of us."

Mrs. Dunn chuckled. "Score for you. The truth is, though, that I don't think I'm really anxious to be invisible. It's a bit too much like snooping, for my taste. And eavesdroppers never hear any good of themselves. What is the practical application of the thing anyway, Professor? What will you do with it?"

"I really haven't considered. We've already shown its value in observing birds. I suppose it would be a fine tool for naturalists, for anyone studying wildlife. But as you know, Dr. Grimes thinks of me as a dreamer, and I guess he's right. I have been very interested in the problems involved in developing the invisibility simulator, but I haven't thought about its uses."

"Maybe it could be used for studying another planet," Danny said. "You could put one in a spaceship and then, instead of landing a man, send him down invisibly to study the place. That way, he wouldn't frighten the people on the planet and he could decide whether it was safe to land."

"An intriguing idea, my boy. Only, we'd have to find another way of powering it, if your spaceship was going to stay in a distant orbit. Microwaves have a limited range."

He and Dan plunged into a technical discussion of laser beams.

"Your eggs are getting cold," said Mrs. Dunn. "Finish up, Dan, for heaven's sake."

"I *am* eating, aren't I?" He quickly scooped up a forkful of eggs and crammed it into his mouth.

"Aren't I?" repeated the Professor. "What kind of English is that?"

"I'm not supposed to say 'ain't,' " Danny replied.

"Why ever not? What's wrong with it? It's only a contraction of 'amn't' or 'am not.' You don't say, 'I are eating,' do you?"

"I guess not."

"You say, 'I am eating,' so you should say 'amn't I?' As a contraction, 'ain't' is no worse than 'couldn't' or 'won't.' "

The Professor raised a finger and seemed about to launch into a long discussion of grammar, but just then the telephone rang.

"It's for you, Professor," said Mrs. Dunn.

He got up and took the phone. "Yes, this is he. You what? Who? . . . I see . . . Yes, I'll be waiting for you. Very well. Good-bye."

He turned to them with a puzzled look. "Somebody named General Gruntle from the Pentagon wants to see me," he said. "He's coming here at once."

"All the way from Washington?" said Mrs. Dunn.

"He's already done that. He was calling from the Midston airfield. I don't know how he got there—as you know, it's a small field and there are no big commercial flights landing there."

"If he came in a military plane—" Mrs. Dunn began.

"That's it!" Danny interrupted. "Sure! I'll bet Dr. Grimes told him about Isit, and he's coming to give you a medal. Oh, boy, Professor! Can I stay and watch?"

"Dan may be right," said Mrs. Dunn. "I can't think of any other reason why a general would come to see you. Oh, heavens, and look at my kitchen! And the rest of the house is filthy—"

"Filthy? You just vacuumed everything yesterday," the Professor protested. "He won't notice a few specks of dust. I'm going out to the lab. When he comes, send him out there."

Dan ran around the table and stopped the Professor before he could get to the kitchen door.

"What about me? I want to see him pin it on you."

"Now, Dan, that's just nonsense," said the Professor. "I'm the last person in the world to get a medal, and if anyone tries to give me one, I'll turn it down anyway. I don't approve of medals. But if you want to come out to the lab with me, you may certainly do so. I want to show you an improvement I've thought of, for the sensory module."

They were busy together over some wiring when Mrs. Dunn opened the lab door and said, "General Gruntle is here, Professor."

To Danny, at first, it seemed as though the room was full of uniforms. He blinked, and saw that there were, in fact, only four. The man in the lead, however, was so imposing that he gave the impression of being a whole regiment.

He was not tall but very wide. The peak of
his cap was covered with gold braid, and more
gold braid decorated his jacket. All across the
front of him there were ribbons and badges of
every color, shape, and size, so that it almost
hurt Danny's eyes to look at him. His face
was mottled with red, and he wore glittering

gold-rimmed glasses that flashed fiercely like the gold braid on his cap.

He was followed by a paler version of himself, another officer with a little less braid, fewer medals, a paler face, and horn-rimmed glasses. This second man had a slight stoop and a rather nervous air. He looked, Danny thought, like a man who was used to being shouted at.

Behind these two came two soldiers, a corporal and a private first class, both wearing the helmets, armbands, and pistols of the military police. They took up positions, one on each side of the door, and stood there with their hands behind their backs.

"Professor Euclid Bullfinch?" said the leader. He had a very loud, resonant voice, and when he spoke, the second man gave a little jump. "I am General Harold Gruntle."

"How do you do?" said the Professor.

"This is my aide, Colonel Twist."

"And this is my—er—assistant, Daniel Dunn," said the Professor.

"I think, perhaps, if you don't mind, the boy had better leave," said the General. "Colonel Twist, take him outside."

Professor Bullfinch raised his eyebrows. He was, ordinarily, the mildest and gentlest of men, but nothing could make him more stubborn than the feeling that he was being bullied. He held up his hand as the Colonel moved.

"I do mind," he said. "Danny is, as I have said, my assistant. The fact that he's a boy has nothing to do with his intelligence. He'll stay right here."

General Gruntle's face became redder than ever. It was obvious that very few people ever disagreed with him. All he said, however, was, "Very well. I'll get right to the point, then."

"Won't you have a seat?" said the Professor. He pulled two stools away from one of the worktables. After a moment's hesitation, the officers sat down. The Professor, with a small, private smile, leaned back against a corner of the bench, pulled out his pipe, and began to fill it.

"Please make yourselves comfortable," he said. "Now, what can I do for you, General?"

"We've learned that you have invented what sounds like a very interesting device— if it's true. Not only interesting, but important. Am I right?"

"I've invented a great many things, General," said the Professor. "Which one are you talking about?"

"I am told you've discovered a way to

make someone invisible. Ordinarily, I'd take that sort of claim with a grain of salt, but the source from which I've learned it is very trustworthy. Very trustworthy, indeed. No less than Dr. A. J. Grimes, head of the Academy of Scientific Research."

"Ah," said the Professor. "I see." Very deliberately, he put a match to his pipe, and after he had puffed it alight, went on, "Well, sir, it's partly true and partly not true. I have not invented a way of making someone invisible. But I have invented a sensory probe which returns signals so that the effect to the user is something like invisibility."

"The same thing. And have you gone beyond the purely theoretical stage?"

"There's the machine itself, right beside you," said the Professor, with a nod of his head.

General Gruntle jumped, as if he had been pinched, and Colonel Twist jumped even more sharply so that he almost fell off his stool.

"That little thing?" snapped the General. "I don't believe it."

"You may try it if you like," said the Professor.

The General looked suspiciously at him. "Are you serious? Here and now?"

"Certainly. Have you ever flown an airplane?"

"I can't say I have."

"Never mind. If Danny could master it, so can you."

General Gruntle scowled. "Do you mean to say you have allowed that boy to use the invisibility machine?"

"Of course. He's very good at it, too."

The General's mouth turned down at the corners. "Dr. Grimes was right, I see. He warned me that you were completely impractical."

The Professor laughed. "Yes, he was right.

Come along, General. I'll show you how to manipulate it."

General Gruntle was nowhere near as good as the children had been at handling the dragonfly. He was stiff and tense, his reflexes were slow, and he couldn't seem to get the knack of floating on the air currents. Twice the dragonfly twirled to the floor. After the second time, the Professor picked it up and carried it around the lab so that the General could see how it worked.

When, at last, General Gruntle was helped out of the helmet and gauntlets, he sat for a time in thought. Then he said, "What's the range of this bug?"

"Dan and I were discussing that very matter when you came in. Not very far, at present. Perhaps twenty-five hundred yards."

"But it might be extended?"

"Possibly. It will take some work."

The General got to his feet. "Professor Bullfinch," he said, "I am going to have to take this machine to Washington. Colonel Twist!" The Colonel leaped up. "Take charge of it."

Before Colonel Twist could do anything, the Professor stepped forward, clapped his hand on the control box, and said, "Stop!"

"Look here—" the General began.

"No, sir," said the Professor. "You look here. You are in my private laboratory, and this machine is my property. You do not have the right to touch it without my permission, and as far as I know, I haven't yet given you my permission."

General Gruntle began huffing with anger. Controlling himself with an effort, he said, in a voice just a little less than a bellow, "You don't seem to understand the importance of this thing to the national defense. You have invented a weapon which will make the army supreme in espionage. Just think of the uses for it! It's a perfect machine for spying. It can be used to penetrate all enemy defenses and with a few modifications could be used to blow up ammunition dumps, ferret out enemy secrets, or even assassinate enemy leaders."

He paused, and another idea struck him. "Even more important, just think of all those people right here at home who don't approve of some of the things we want to do. With a few thousand of these machines, we could keep an eye on any such disloyal elements. Why, no one could do or say a thing that we wouldn't know about. It would put us in the driver's seat, that's what it would do. It's your patriotic duty to turn the thing over to me."

The Professor scratched his nose thoughtfully with his pipe stem. "Please calm down, General," he said. "I admit that what you say puts a different light on my invention. I never thought of it as a weapon. It's true, it might have some uses that way. But even more to the point, I certainly never thought of it as a way someone could spy on American citizens. That seems to me a violation of our right to privacy."

"That's not what I meant—" General Gruntle began.

"Perhaps Isit would be a valuable weapon," the Professor went on, as if the other hadn't spoken. "But what you say makes me realize how dangerous it would be if it fell into the wrong hands. I don't necessarily mean you. I mean someone—anyone—who wanted to find out what everyone was thinking and doing so that he could have the power to control us all. It's just because I *am* patriotic that I see how bad that sort of thing could be. Surely, you can see it, too, General?"

General Gruntle opened his mouth several times before he could get any words out. Then he roared, "Rubbish! Ridiculous! You talk like one of those long-haired, wild-eyed, dreamy idealists. Come down to earth, man!

I tell you it's your duty to give up the invisibility machine."

"No," said the Professor. "At any rate, not now. Not until I've had a chance to think about it."

"We'll see about that," said the General.

He had taken off his cap so that he could operate the machine. Now, he snatched it up and clapped it on his head.

"I'm returning to Washington for a consultation at the highest level. I expect to get full authorization to secure the machine and everything connected with its research and operation. In the interests of national security, I shall have to ask you to promise me not to remove the machine—or anything else—from this laboratory until I return."

The Professor hesitated. Then he said, "Until you return. Very well. I agree to that. It will give me time to consider the matter."

General Gruntle turned to his aide. "Colonel, I leave you in charge here. See that all windows and doors are locked. There are only two doors, eh? Station Corporal Blevitch at one and Private Ferris at the other. Their orders are to admit no one—no one at all, for any reason—to the laboratory."

"Yes, sir. But sir, but sir," said Colonel Twist, "excuse me, sir, but are they supposed to be on twenty-four hour duty? I mean, how are they going to eat or sleep?"

"That's their problem, Colonel," snapped the General. "And yours. I'll be at the Pentagon if there's an emergency. I expect to be back here within twenty-four hours, anyway."

"Just a moment, General," the Professor put in. "Do you mean to say I can't go into my own laboratory? I've already given you my word—"

"I'm taking no chances, Professor. If I've heard about your invention, the Other Side may have heard also."

"The Other Side?" said the Professor, in surprise.

"Them," said General Gruntle mysteriously. "Just let 'em try to get in and steal it, that's all. Twist! Give those men orders to shoot to kill if they see or hear anything suspicious."

With that, he gave the Professor a snappy salute and strode out of the room.

8

An Emergency Conference

The Professor and Danny stood gaping after the General. After a moment, they became aware of a peculiar rasping noise. It was Colonel Twist, clearing his throat.

"Ah, yes, Colonel, what is it?" asked the Professor.

"Er—er—excuse me, Professor Bullfinch," said the Colonel, "but I'll have to ask you to lab the leave—er—leave the laboratory."

It was obvious that he was feeling jittery. Not surprising, Danny considered, in someone whose superior was General Gruntle.

"That's quite all right," said the Professor, in a soothing tone. "We're going. Just one thing. Surely you're not going to make these two soldiers stand guard at the doors for the next twenty-four hours?"

"Yes, sir, I am. You heard the General. I haven't any choice," said the Colonel unhappily.

"Well, we'll give them chairs so they can be comfortable. As for you, you can use the spare bedroom. I'll arrange with Mrs. Dunn to give you all something to eat. Come on, Dan."

Shaking his head, the Professor went along the hall to his study. Here, leaning against the wall, was his cello case. The Professor was a very good amateur performer. He opened the case, rosined his bow, tuned the instrument, and began to play the slow movement from one of the Bach suites. Dan stood and listened for a while in silence.

Then he said, "It's not fair, Professor. What are you going to do about it?"

"I'm going to sit here for a while and finish this piece of music, my boy," said the Professor. "Would you be good enough to get a couple of chairs for those soldiers? They're going to be awfully tired after a few hours."

"But Professor—"

"Not now, Dan. I want to listen to myself play. I need some calming."

And that was all that could be gotten out of him. After a bit, Danny left him and got two folding aluminum armchairs from the garden shed. He gave one to PFC Ferris, who was at the back door and who said, "Thanks a lot, kid. I'm just glad it isn't raining." Then Dan went around through the house and gave the other chair to Corporal Blevitch, who promptly sat down in it with a sigh, tipped it back against the wall, pulled his helmet forward over his eyes, and lit a cigarette.

Colonel Twist was walking up and down the hall with his hands behind his back. He looked at the Corporal with annoyance, but did nothing.

"Er—ah—" he said to Danny. "Where's your mother, sonny?"

Danny hated being called sonny, and he didn't much care for Colonel Twist, but he remembered his manners.

"Come with me," he said. "She's out in the kitchen. I guess I'd better break it to her that you're going to stay here."

Mrs. Dunn was a calm sort of person, and she took without blinking the news that she now had three guests.

"We're glad to have you, of course," she said politely, "but I don't think I understand what it's all about. It has something to do with Professor Bullfinch's new invention, I suppose?"

96

"It is a highly important seek-topret—er—" Colonel Twist began. "I mean top-secret—"

"They want to grab it for the army," Danny broke in. "The Colonel and the soldiers are guarding it, while the General gets some kind of okay from Washington."

"I see." Mrs. Dunn's voice took on a tone Danny knew well. He had last heard it when he had managed to spill a beaker of nitric acid over a mahogany table top. "I think I ought to tell you, Colonel, that I don't approve. However, as you are a guest in my house, we won't discuss it. Since there are three more of you for dinner, and since I didn't actually invite you, you can make yourself useful. Sit down and start shelling those peas."

"Yes, ma'am," said Colonel Twist meekly. It was plain he was used to being ordered about.

Dan went out, and after thinking for a bit, ran next door to the Millers'. He and Irene were always in and out of each other's houses, and he marched in without bothering to knock. He found Irene reading in a big armchair, her legs over one of its arms, her back against the other, with a big glass of chocolate milk within comfortable reach on the floor.

"Hi," she said. "Have you ever read *She, the Adventuress?* It's neat."

"Never mind that now," said Dan. "Is your mother home?"

"She's at a meeting of the League of Women Voters. She's the vice-president, you know."

"Good. We've got to have an emergency conference. I'll call Joe."

He dialed the number, and Irene returned to her book.

"What's this all about?" she asked, when he hung up.

"I'll tell you when Joe gets here. He'll be over in a couple of minutes. Is there any more chocolate milk?"

"Sure. In the refrigerator. Go get it. I want to finish this chapter."

Joe arrived on his bike very shortly. He left it on the lawn, came in by the back door, and surveyed his friends, both busy with books and glasses of milk.

"A party," he said. "How nice. Are you giving out presents, too?"

"Go grab yourself a glass of chocolate milk if you want to. Then we have to talk," said Danny.

"And a cookie?"

"There aren't any," said Irene.

"Then I don't know if I'll stay," Joe grumbled, shaking his head.

He went off to the kitchen, muttering something about "... trying to starve a poor undernourished kid ..." When he returned, in addition to a glass of chocolate milk, he had a large piece of bread and butter sprinkled with brown sugar. He sat himself on the floor. Dan put aside Dr. Miller's copy of *An Approach to Modern Physics,* which he had been leafing through, and sat up straight.

"It's about Professor Bullfinch," he began solemnly. "He can't get into his own laboratory."

"You mean he lost the key?" asked Joe.

"I mean he isn't allowed to. The army won't let him in. And what's more, they're going to take Isit away."

The grins faded from his friends' faces as they stared at him.

"You're joking!" exclaimed Irene.

Danny shook his head.

"But why? I don't get it. How can they do that?"

"They claim it's going to help them spy on everybody. The Professor doesn't think they should use it that way."

"But maybe they're right," said Joe. "I mean, if the Professor had invented some kind of weapon, like a giant cannon or a death ray, it would help the army if there was a war, so—"

"But Isit isn't a weapon, and there isn't a war," said Danny. "What General Gruntle said was that this would let the army keep an eye on people here in America, so that they could find out what everybody was saying or doing. My gosh, I wouldn't want somebody snooping on me all the time. Would you?"

"They might find out some awfully peculiar stuff," said Joe. He shivered. "No. I guess I wouldn't."

"There's no telling who would be doing the snooping, either. Suppose it was somebody like Snitcher?" Danny went on. "Anyway, that's not the main point. The thing is, Isit belongs to the Professor. He invented it. They don't have any right to just walk in and take it. He should have the right to say what he wants to do with his own invention."

Irene was sitting with her chin in her hand, pondering. She said slowly, "The Professor got the stuff to invent it with from Dr. Grimes."

"That's right," said Danny. "But that doesn't make Isit belong to Dr. Grimes. Suppose I got some paper and ink from you and wrote out a science report. Would it be yours or mine?"

"Okay," said Irene. "I agree."

"And anyway, it was Dan who discovered how to make the stuff work," said Joe. "Even if it was an accident. So it's as much his as it is Dr. Grimes's."

"It isn't mine at all, any more than it's Dr. Grimes's," Danny said. "And I don't think anybody has the right to just walk in and keep the Professor from making up his own mind about what to do with it."

"Why doesn't the Professor just go into the lab anyway and take Isit?" said Joe. "Do you think the soldiers would really stop him? Would they shoot him? I'll bet they wouldn't dare."

"It's not that." Dan threw out his hands. "He promised he wouldn't, that's why. He promised he'd wait until General Gruntle got back from Washington. He said it would give him time to think about it."

Irene stood up. "What about you, Danny?"

"What about me?"

"Did you make any promises?"

"Me? Of course not. They didn't ask—" Danny's expression changed. "Oho! I see what you mean. You didn't make any promises either. Neither did Joe."

"That's right," Irene said firmly. "There's nothing to stop *us* from going into the laboratory and taking Isit away. Is there?"

"Nothing but the whole U.S. Army," groaned Joe. "I knew there was going to be trouble the minute the whole thing started. I knew it, I knew it."

"Oh, calm down, Joe," said Dan. "What about it? Are we all in this together?"

"Of course I'm in," Irene said. "It was my idea, wasn't it?"

"Joe?"

"All right," said Joe, with a comical look of despair. "Just promise me one thing."

"What?"

"That you'll write to me when I'm in jail."

9

The Theft of Isit

The three friends lurked in the shrubbery at the edge of the lawn, studying the back of Danny's house. Everything was deceptively quiet and peaceful. The leaves stirred gently now and then, whispering to each other. The nooning sun warmed the clapboard of the old house and picked out the bright line of the rain gutter along the edge of the newer structure, which was the Professor's laboratory. At the door of the lab, Corporal Blevitch sprawled in his chair, his legs stretched out, his hands folded over his stomach. A robin hopped nearby, listening for worms, hardly bothering to watch the soldier.

"If we had some dynamite," Joe mused, "we could blow the door open."

"Uh-huh," said Danny. "That's a real Joe idea. And then we rush in with our machine guns blazing . . ."

"All right, if you don't like that, here's another one. We disguise ourselves and go in to read the meter or fix the plumbing. Then when we're inside—"

"Yes? Then what?"

"Then I don't know what," said Joe.

They lay on their stomachs, peering out silently. Irene said, "If we could cut a hole in the roof, we could climb in that way."

"Poofle!" said Danny.

"Poofle?" Joe repeated. "I like that. What does it mean?"

"It means we're just talking and not getting anywhere. If we could cut a hole in the—"

He stopped.

"Go on," said Irene. "You obviously have some idea."

"Wait a sec. I want to think."

He rested his chin on his arms, pondering, and he was so still that a small, passing butterfly took him for a rock and rested for a moment on his elbow.

Then he said, "As long as that soldier is

guarding the door, he can't see around the corner of the building."

"Now that," said Joe, "is what I call an astute observation. But I don't see that it gets us anywhere."

"Around the corner of the building is the window to the Professor's office in the lab," Danny continued patiently.

"But all the windows are locked," Irene objected. "You told us that General What's-his-name gave the orders for it."

"No, I see what Danny means," said Joe. "We cut a hole in that window and sneak in and get Isit. But the soldier would hear us cutting the hole, wouldn't he?"

"I wasn't thinking of cutting any holes in windows," Danny said, shaking his head. "I was thinking of breaking holes in windows. Or rather, breaking *a* hole in *a* window."

"I'm lost," said Joe. "I don't understand."

"Okay," Danny said. "Listen. Suppose we're playing baseball on the lawn and somebody hits a ball through one of the windows of the lab. Then we ask the soldier if we can just go in and get it back."

"And we steal Isit—?"

"Don't be silly. We can't walk out in front of him with it. No, but whoever goes in for the ball unlocks the side window of the office. Right?"

"I could do that," Irene said. "I can look more innocent than you boys can."

"Okay. Then this evening, when it's getting dark but isn't too dark for us to see what we're doing, we open that window, go in and get Isit, and bring it out that way."

"Suppose the soldier happens to glance in through one of the other windows?"

"We'll have to be sure he doesn't. That means that one of us will have to keep him busy while the other two are inside."

"I'll be that one," said Joe. "I've got an idea how to do it. But what about the other soldier, the one inside the back door?"

"He can't see into the lab, can he? And if we're as quiet as mice, he won't hear anything through that door. It's a good thick one."

"It might work," said Irene.

"It's got to work," said Danny. "We won't get a second chance. I'll get a bat and a ball and meet you on the lawn in a couple of minutes."

When they met again, they tried hard to make everything look natural. They laughed —a little too loudly—and talked to each other in voices which, if Corporal Blevitch had been listening carefully, would have sounded peculiarly strained. He only yawned, however, and watched them with dull eyes.

The three tossed the baseball back and forth a few times, and then Dan motioned his friends in close.

"It's going to be tricky," he said, in a low tone. "We'll have to do it the first time. We can't keep hitting the ball toward the house or it'll look suspicious. Who's going to do it?"

"You're a better batter than I am," Irene said generously.

"Well, honestly, I guess I am. And I've worked out in my head just what the force and trajectory have to be. The ball will have to fly off at an angle of exactly thirteen degrees. What we'd better do is this. Suppose Joe gets up and pretends to bat a couple of times—"

"What do you mean 'pretends'?" said Joe indignantly. "You're talking about the Midston Slugger."

"All right, Joe *really* bats a couple of times so it'll look like we're really playing or practicing. Then Irene can pitch one to me, and I'll try to send it through the window."

He walked back toward the house, and Joe got ready, with Irene behind him as catcher. Danny pitched an easy, slow ball and, as usual, Joe closed his eyes and swung.

Crack! The ball flew lazily over Dan's head, straight through the top pane of one of the windows, making a beautiful round hole from which glass fell tinkling.

Danny was so surpised that he stood motionless, with his mouth hanging open. Irene uttered a shriek. As for Joe, he dropped the bat, fell flat on his face, and began laughing hysterically.

Irene was the first to recover. "Shut up, you idiot," she whispered. "You're not supposed to laugh when you break a window."

"I ca-ca-can't help it," he gasped. "Trajectory! Angle of thirteen degrees—!"

Irene stepped over Joe and hurried to Corporal Blevitch, who had been thoroughly waked up by the sound of breaking glass and was grinning broadly.

"You kids are gonna be in trouble," he said to Irene.

"Oh, I know, sir," Irene said, looking pathetic. "We'll have to tell the Professor and he'll be so angry. But we can't play any more without our ball. Can't I just go in and get it?"

"Nobody's supposed to go in there," said the Corporal.

"Not even just for a teeny little minute? Just to get our ball back?"

Irene's shoulders slumped, and she looked up into the soldier's face with swimming eyes. "How can you be so *mean?*" she quavered.

She started to turn away, and Corporal Blevitch said hastily, "Wait a minute. All right. Go in and get your ball and come right out again. But don't touch nothing."

"What would I touch?" Irene said. "All I want is the ball so we can go on playing."

The Corporal unlocked the door and pushed it open. Irene darted inside. At the same time, Dan called, "Hey, Corporal!"

Corporal Blevitch's attention was turned to him. "What?"

"Gee, thanks a lot for letting her in. Would you like a pitcher of ice-cold lemonade? It's pretty hot out here."

"That would be great, kid."

"I'll go get it now, while we're waiting."

He ran off to the kitchen. As the Corporal turned back to the door, Irene came out, smiling and holding up the baseball.

"Thank you," she said.

"That's okay." He shut the door and turned the key.

Irene went to Joe, who was sitting up, wiping the tears of laughter from his eyes.

"You nut," she said, laughing also, in spite of herself.

"How did it go?"

"All done."

Danny reappeared with the lemonade and a glass, which he gave to the soldier. Then he joined the others. He raised his eyebrows at Irene, who nodded.

"Good," he said. "We'll have to keep playing so it doesn't look funny. And since Joe has already made the home run of the day, he can chase balls for a while."

That evening after dinner Colonel Twist made his rounds. He had visited the two sentries every couple of hours during the afternoon and had spent the rest of the time in the living room, reading old magazines and watching television. He had switched the men's posts late in the afternoon, putting Corporal Blevitch inside the back door and PFC Ferris outside the front door, so that they'd have a change of scene. Now, as dusk was closing in, he checked on them once more.

PFC Ferris was walking back and forth outside the lab to get the stiffness out of his legs. He came to attention and saluted as the Colonel appeared.

"Everything all right, Ferris?"

"Yes, sir."

"Had your dinner?"

"Yes, sir. That Professor guy brought it out to me on a tray. Great food, too."

Colonel Twist unlocked the door and peered into the lab. He made sure Isit was still where it had been left, on the workbench. Then he turned on the outside light over the door and locked up again.

"Keep your eyes open," he told the soldier. "I'll check again in two hours."

After he had gone, PFC Ferris opened his shirt collar, took off his helmet and wiped his forehead, and then began pacing once more from one end of the building to the other. Now and then he slapped at a mosquito.

The air was gray and the shadows under the trees and bushes had thickened so that the wink of an occasional firefly blazed out like the sudden glow of a lighted cigarette. A bat skittered overhead. There was an air of mystery about the darkening garden, and it was not surprising that the soldier should be startled when a figure suddenly appeared in the light that hung above the doorway.

"Who's that?" snapped Ferris.

"Joe," came the answer.

Ferris went up to him. "Who are you?

You're not the kid who brought me the chair."

"No," said Joe. "I'm the other one."

"What other one?"

"The one who didn't bring you a chair."

PFC Ferris shrugged. For all he knew there were several children living in the house.

"What do you want?"

"Nothing. I've been working on a poem, and I work best when I can walk around and think."

"You mean you're writing a poem?" Ferris raised his eyebrows. "How come? You a poet or something?"

"Mostly something," Joe said modestly. "But I do make up poems. I wrote one this afternoon about a general. Would you like to hear it?"

"Sure. Go ahead."

Joe cleared his throat, and began to recite:

> "My gallant men march forward,"
> Said General Delay.
> "And I'll be right behind you
> To lead you to the fray."

"Where's this fray place?" asked PFC Ferris.

"It's a word we poets use. It means 'battle,' " said Joe.

"I get it."

> The gallant troops marched
>   forward;
> Their hearts went pitter-pat.
> The guns went *boom!* They turned
>   and ran,
> And stamped the General flat.

> The moral of this story is
> That war can kill you dead.
> To be a happy general
> Stay safely home in bed.

PFC Ferris roared with mirth. "That's great," he said. "Just like a general, too. No kidding, did you really make that up yourself?"

"Sure."

"You're one smart kid. Man, I have to learn that. Could you write it out for me?"

"I'll be glad to," said Joe. He pulled his little notebook—he was never without it—from his back pocket, turned to a blank page, sat down in the folding chair, and began to write. PFC Ferris watched over his shoulder.

While this was going on, Dan and Irene

had made their way into the lab. They had waited in the shadows near the kitchen door until they heard the soldier call to Joe. Then, they had gone swiftly around to the window of the Professor's office and silently pushed it up. They had climbed in like cats.

"Do you think he can see us in here with that outside light on?" Irene had whispered.

"Joe's keeping him busy," Danny had replied. "And anyway, when there's a light outside and none inside, you can't see much through a window into a room."

Working as fast as they could, they had

carried the helmet and gauntlets and control box to the window. Danny had shoved the dragonfly into his pocket. Once, he had stumbled, and they froze, waiting, but neither PFC Ferris nor Corporal Blevitch, who was dozing in his chair in the hall, heard anything.

Now, as Joe carefully wrote down his poem, taking as long as he could with it, Irene slipped out of the window. Danny reached the parts of Isit through to her, and then followed, pulling down the window behind him. Then, as they had agreed, he gave an owl's hoot to let Joe know that they were out.

"What was that?" said PFC Ferris.

"What was what?"

"That noise. It sounded like a cat being drowned."

"It was an owl," Joe said solemnly, finishing his writing. "The Red-headed Lesser Screech Owl. Very common around here. There you are, there's the poem."

"Thanks, buster. Wait'll I read this to my buddies. They won't believe a kid wrote it."

"Well, he did—I mean, I did," said Joe. "So long. I've got to get back to work on my other poem."

He ambled away, and as soon as he was around the corner and out of sight, he ducked into the darkness of the big old lilac bush between the Professor's house and that of the Millers. Dan and Irene were already crouching there with Isit on the ground between them.

"We did it!" Joe whispered. "Now what?"

"Now we hide it," Dan replied.

"Where?" said Irene. "Where will it be safe?"

Danny giggled. "In the last place they'll think of looking for it," he said. "In my house."

10

Danny Overlooks Something

Irene's "What?" came out as a bat squeak of astonishment.

"Do you mean—" Joe began, in a normal voice, and quickly changed it to a whisper. "Do you mean you want to carry this back into the lab?"

"Of course not. Who said anything about the lab? We'll put it in the cellar."

Danny peered at his friends' faces in the gloom. He could see them only as glimmering white blurs. "Listen," he said. "As soon as the Colonel finds out Isit is gone, he's going to figure some spy crept in and stole it. That's why General Gruntle told him to lock the doors and windows—so that the Other Side, he said, wouldn't be able to get it. He sure isn't going to think the spy hid Isit in the same house he took it out of."

"I hope you're right," said Joe. "But nothing would really surprise me anymore."

They carried the control box, helmet, and gauntlets to the kitchen door. The kitchen was dark, and they crept in and made their way to the cellar door. They could hear the television going in the living room. Dan snapped on the light switch at the head of the cellar stairs, and they carried their burdens down to the basement and into a bin which had once held coal but now was used for storage. There was a scooter Dan had used when he was small, a broken radio, an old electric motor, cartons full of dusty glass jars, pans with holes in them, and outgrown toys. Among this litter, they deposited Isit, and Dan carefully covered it with an empty cardboard box.

Upstairs again, Dan turned on the kitchen light and took some bottles of soda out of the refrigerator. Silently, the three toasted each other. They were all feeling a little subdued and more than a little uneasy, now that they had actually accomplished their mission.

"Well," Irene said, at last, "I've got to go

home. I'll see you tomorrow and find out if anything happened."

"Me, too," sad Joe. "Are you going to tell Professor Bullfinch?"

Danny bit his lip. "Gosh, I don't know," he said. "I never thought of that."

"Maybe you'd better think of it," Joe said.

When his friends had gone, Dan went into the living room. His mother was placidly knitting, with only one eye on a program about Henry VIII. He watched her for a moment and then said, "Where's Professor Bullfinch, Mom?"

"In his den, reading, I think, dear."

Danny had already guessed that but was

stalling out of pure nervousness. He had half-hoped the Professor might have gone out, so that he could postpone telling him about Isit. After all, the Professor might not approve.

Dragging his feet, he went along the hall. He nodded to Corporal Blevitch, who was reading a comic book. He knocked at the door of the Professor's den, and at the Professor's "Come in," reluctantly entered.

"What is it, Dan?" the Professor said, closing his book on one finger to keep his place.

"Um . . ." said Danny. "Well, I was wondering. What have you decided? About Isit, I mean."

"I've been thinking it over," said the Professor. "Before I say anything, I'd like you to tell me what *you* think."

Dan said promptly, "I don't think you should give up the machine."

"Why not?"

"I've been thinking about it, too. Do you remember when we were talking about it this morning at breakfast? Wow! it seems like a million years ago. Mom said it would be a good way for her to keep an eye on me, to find out whether I did my homework. She was just joking, but man, it scared me. I started thinking—I'd never have any privacy. And General Gruntle's way, you'd never know when somebody was standing right next to you, watching and listening to everything that was going on."

The Professor nodded. "I remember that. I agree with you. It seems to me the whole problem is this: Who will be using Isit? A machine is just a machine—*it* can't be good or bad, it depends on who's using it. An automobile is a good machine for getting you somewhere in a hurry, but in the wrong hands it can kill you."

He laid aside his book. "Do you know what decided me? I have been thinking of Isit in the hands of General Gruntle. Maybe it's just because I don't like him, but I wouldn't want *him* hovering invisibly behind me."

"Then you've made up your mind not to give it to them?"

"Yes, I think so. However, there's one great difficulty—"

He was not allowed to finish. The door flew open with a bang. There stood Colonel Twist, red in the face.

He pointed a finger at the Professor and snapped, "If you did it—!"

"Just a moment," Professor Bullfinch said, holding up his hand. "Please calm down, Colonel. I don't know what you're talking about."

"That machine. The invisibilamy—invelebil—invisibility! It's gone! That's what."

Colonel Twist all but sobbed. "Nobody has gone past the sentries. Nobody! How could—?" He caught himself. "Is there another one? Tell me the truth, now. Did someone else make himself invisible and go into the laboratory—?"

"No, sir. There is no other invisibility simulator," said the Professor. "And I assure you, I didn't break my promise. I've been sitting right here all evening. The soldier out in the hall can tell you that. When did you find out it was gone?"

"Just now. It must have happened within the last half-hour. I checked the sentries at eight-thirty and saw the machine in the laboratory myself. That was less than an hour ago. A few minutes ago, I suddenly felt very uneasy and decided to make an early check. The minute I put the light on, I could see that it was gone."

"No one could have taken it without being seen," said the Professor.

"It's impossible!" Colonel Twist cried. "It's a diabolical plot. Foreign spies! How did they do it? How did they know?"

He stalked to the table and snatched up the telephone. "You sit right there and don't move," he said to the Professor. Quickly, he dialed a number.

"This is Colonel Twist," he said. "Get me General Gruntle . . . What? In a meeting? I don't care where he is, get him. Emergency priority."

A few moments later, the General's loud voice could be heard clearly at the other end of the line. "Gruntle here. What's the trouble?"

"The trouble is we have some trouble, sir," said the wretched Colonel. Large beads of sweat began forming on his forehead. "We have this trouble—about the invisibility simulator."

"Spit it out, will you?"

"I'm afraid it's gone."

The telephone buzzed and vibrated like a nest of angry hornets.

"We did keep watch, sir," stuttered Colonel Twist. "The sentries never left their posts except when they left them because they had to . . . and I took over until they got back. No, sir, nobody went in at all. Honest, General, I swear it! Not a soul. Well, I know it didn't walk away by itself, sir. No, the Professor's right here. I'm sure he didn't take it.

Yes, sir, somebody from outside—that's what

I thought, too. What? I'm not supposed to think? Yes, sir."

He fell silent, and after a bit, the General's voice could be heard again. Colonel Twist said, "Yes, sir," several times, and then hung up.

"This is a very grave situation." he said to the Professor. "I have orders that you are not to leave the house. Nobody is to leave the house until General Gruntle gets here."

"What?" said the Professor. "Are you serious?"

"Yes, sir, I'm afraid I am. It is a matter of national security. I am authorized to call in the National Guard to surround the house. General Gruntle will bring an intelligence team with him when he comes. Furthermore, nothing in your laboratory is to be touched or moved, and nobody is to be allowed to enter either the lab or the house. After all, we don't know what else you might have in there that might be important."

"This is preposterous!" said the Professor. "You have no right to keep us prisoners in our own house."

"I'm sorry, Professor," said Colonel Twist. He looked not only sorry but a little sick. However, he was much more afraid of General Gruntle than of the Professor. "It's no longer a local affair. The General is discussing the whole matter with the Chief of Intelligence. If an enemy power has stolen your invisibility machine—"

"Nonsense!" the Professor interrupted. "I don't know exactly what's happened, or who has—"

He stopped short, for at that moment his gaze had fallen on Danny.

Danny had been doing his best to make himself as invisible as he could without any machinery. He had pressed himself back into a corner when Colonel Twist entered the room and had kept perfectly quiet, not even breathing loudly. But as the Professor had spoken, he could not help staring at him, and his silence and wide-eyed look had given him away as plainly as if he had told everything. Professor Bullfinch, after all, was as close to Dan as a father.

"Hm," said the Professor.

Colonel Twist had noticed nothing. He said, "I told you I'm sorry, but that's the way things have got to be. I'm going to phone the local National Guard commander now. Please don't try to leave the house—that goes for the boy, too, and Mrs. Dunn. I'd have to have one of my men stop you, and I don't want to do that."

The Professor sank back in his chair and put the tips of his fingers together. "Very well," he said. "Would you mind using the phone in the hall? I haven't anything else to say to you."

Colonel Twist looked more miserable than ever. "I'm sorry about this, sir, I really am," he repeated. "I'll explain things to Mrs. Dunn."

"You won't enjoy *that*," said the Professor, unable to keep from smiling.

When the door had closed behind Colonel Twist, the Professor took out his pipe. Keeping his voice low, he said to Danny, "What on earth made you do it?"

"Do what?" said Danny.

"Come, now, Dan. You know what I'm talking about. Why did you take Isit?"

"Well," Danny replied, "we thought it wasn't right for them to have it."

"We? I might have known. The other two were in on it, too."

Danny nodded. "If you don't approve, Professor, why didn't you tell Colonel Twist?"

"I'm as bad as you are. I don't think it's right for them to have it, either. Have you forgotten what we were talking about before he came in?"

Professor Bullfinch looked down at his

pipe. Slowly, he got out his pouch and began to pack tobacco into the bowl.

"How on earth did you manage to get it out right under their noses?" he said. "Never mind, don't tell me now. There's one important detail you overlooked. I'm afraid all your work has gone for nothing. You left something behind which is just as important as the machine itself."

"What?"

"My notes," replied the Professor. "All my notes about Isit are still in the laboratory, and with those notes anyone can build another model."

11

The Last Flight
of the Dragonfly

Danny gazed at the Professor in dismay. "I never thought of that," he said. "As soon as General Gruntle comes, they'll find the notes. So everything we did was a waste of time."

He slumped back against the wall.

The Professor stood up and clapped him on the back. "Buck up, Dan," he said. "Of course it wasn't a waste. We've got Isit. Now all we have to do is get the notes, or else destroy them."

"Easy," said Danny gloomily. "Maybe Joe was on the right track. He said we ought to get some dynamite and blow the place up."

"How *did* you youngsters get Isit out of the laboratory?" asked the Professor.

Danny explained what they had done. "That window is still unlocked," he concluded. "Or anyway, Colonel Twist didn't say anything about it, so I guess they haven't noticed it. Maybe I can sneak in that way a little later tonight."

Professor Bullfinch shook his head. "The Colonel said he's going to have the house surrounded by soldiers. I suspect they'll be here very soon. But in any case, Dan, in order to sneak in through that window, you'd have to go outside. And I'm sure he will stop you if you try to do that."

"Oh, yeah. I forgot."

"And now that I mention it," the Professor went on, looking unhappy, "once the General arrives, they'll make a thorough inspection of the lab. They'll find that unlocked window and then they may put two and two together and figure out that you and Joe and Irene stole Isit."

"And then you'll be in trouble, too," said Danny. "I did it again! I just went ahead and acted without thinking. I should have left things as they were."

"No, my boy, don't say that," the Professor said. "It's better to try to act to put something right when you know it's wrong, than to sit back without doing anything. At least, you can say you tried."

"I've got to get into the lab, somehow," Danny said, smacking his fist into his palm. "If I can destroy the notes, it won't matter what they find out later. Maybe if you could turn off all the lights in the house, I could slip out in the dark——"

"Hm. I might go to the cellar and throw the main switch."

"Yes, or short-circuit the line, and then ... and— Oh!"

He hit himself on the forehead. "I think I've got it! Professor! Where are the notes?"

"You mean exactly? They're on the work-table next to where the control box was."

"What do they look like? Were they in a notebook?"

"No, they're a sheaf of loose papers. I hadn't yet bound them in a cover."

"Great! Now all we have to do is get down to the cellar without being seen."

"What are you planning, Dan?" said the Professor.

"When Irene was taking her turn with Isit, last week, you told us the dragonfly was very tough but that it would burn easily. I'm going to use it to set fire to your notes."

"I don't understand—" the Professor began, but Danny was already on his way out of the room. With a shrug of resignation, Professor Bullfinch followed him.

Corporal Blevitch was standing before the lab door looking more alert than before. There was no sign of Colonel Twist. Danny went into the living room. Mrs. Dunn still sat with her knitting before the television set. She glanced up as her son and the Professor entered.

"Have you seen Colonel Twist, Mom?" Danny asked.

"Yes. He told me your machine had disappeared, and I said I wasn't surprised that an invisibility machine had become invisible. He gave me his orders. I presume they're the same ones he's given you."

"I'm afraid he's serious, Mrs. Dunn," said the Professor.

"So am I," Mrs. Dunn replied. "I told him that I didn't plan to go out tonight anyway. But I'd like to see them keep me inside tomorrow, when I want to do my shopping."

There was a steely glint in her eyes as she returned to her knitting.

With a grin, Danny beckoned to the Professor, and they went into the hall. As they did so, they heard the roar of an engine in the street. They started toward the front door, but Colonel Twist was there before them. He pulled the door open, and they saw that an army truck had drawn up before the house and soldiers were jumping out of it. A sergeant hastened to salute the Colonel.

"Quick!" Danny whispered to the Professor. "Now's our chance, while he's telling them what to do."

He led the way into the kitchen. Without turning on the lights, he took a flashlight from a drawer and started down the cellar steps. The Professor followed, closing the cellar door behind him. Danny shielded the flashlight with one hand so that only enough of the beam showed to keep them from stumbling.

He pulled away the cardboard box under which Isit was concealed. Outside, the footsteps of the soldiers could be heard at the side of the house.

"Open the cellar window," Dan said. The Professor did so.

Dan plugged the cable of the machine into an outlet. The Professor snapped on the switch and set the controls. Then he helped Dan into the helmet and gauntlets. They did this without using the flashlight so that no glimmer of light would betray them.

In the darkness, Dan had a hard time adjusting through the lenses of the dragonfly to the vague shapes that loomed around him in the cellar.

"Professor," he said, "you'd better give me a start. Put the dragonfly on the windowsill."

The cellar window was on a level with the grass. The Professor picked up the bug and thrust it outside. Dan closed his eyes for a minute or two, and when he opened them, the starlight and the lights from the windows of the house were enough to enable him to see his way. He launched the dragonfly into the air.

The dark masses of shrubbery and trees flitted past him. Then he was in the open, above the lawn behind the house. Yellow light spilled from the laboratory windows and lay along the grass. There were two men with PFC Ferris outside the lab, and another man in the shadows around the corner of the house. Danny realized that he must have just missed the latter as he began his flight.

He made a wide circle over the lawn, and glided more slowly back toward the house. All the lights in the lab were on, but there was no one inside. He blew out a breath of relief, for that had been the one weak point in his plan. However, he knew it was possible that at any moment Colonel Twist might decide to send someone in to keep an eye on things. He would have to act quickly.

The hole Joe had made in the window that morning had never been patched. Dan angled down toward it, slowing his speed still more. As it drew nearer, he had an instant of panic wondering whether it would be large enough to allow the dragonfly's wings to pass. There was just enough room. Dan floated through neatly.

He perched on a shelf, from which he could survey the room. On the stone-topped workbench below him, he could see the little pile of papers covered with the Professor's scrawling handwriting. Nearby stood the lamp, its cord trailing across the top of the table.

There was a folder of paper matches on another table beside a bunsen burner. The dragonfly's claws were incapable of so complicated an action as opening the cover, tearing out a match, or striking it. But Dan had something quite different in mind. He swooped down, picked up the matches, and dropped them on the table on the pile of notes just at the edge of the top sheet of paper. He seized the lamp cord and, after a struggle, succeeded in dragging it a little way over so that it lay across the notes and next to the folder of matches.

Then, grasping the lamp cord with the sharp steel claws, he set to work to pierce it. The insulation was tough, and at first he could hardly make a dent in it. He opened and closed the claws, feeling the hard smooth material under his fingers. The sweat formed on his face and dropped from his nose. The strange, mixed-up feeling so typical of being in the dragonfly—seeing the base of the lamp rising like a tree above his head and at the same time knowing that he was in the cellar with the Professor standing beside him—was stronger than ever.

He heard the voices of the soldiers outside the lab windows. He knew that if they looked in they would never notice the dragonfly on the table, and yet he was spurred to work harder than ever. And at last, he felt the insulation give way.

He clenched his fists. The steel claws bit down and touched the wires inside the insulation. There was a bright flash, as the electric current shorted through the claws. The clear plastic of the dragonfly's body burst into flame.

It had not occurred to Dan that he would feel the pain of the burning. Involuntarily, he snatched his hands away from the controls. But they were still in the gauntlets, and he could still feel the fierce, terrible heat. In the same breath, he realized that he must not stop now; there was one thing more to do. Seizing the controls again and setting his teeth against the pain, he opened the claws and gave the dragonfly a last, powerful forward boost which brought it on top of the folder of matches.

The world seemed to explode in a billow of fire. There was one more short, searing pang, and then every sensation vanished and Danny was in darkness.

At first, he thought he had fainted. Then, slowly, he understood that the dragonfly had been destroyed and all his sensory contact with it had been lost. The vision screens in the helmet had gone black, and in the gauntlets he now felt nothing but the material of which they were made.

"It's finished, Professor," he said, in a weak voice.

He began to struggle out of the gauntlets. The Professor assisted him and took the helmet from his head.

"Are the notes burned?" said the Professor.

"They must be. I shorted the lamp wires, and when the dragonfly caught on fire I flew it into a pack of matches I put on top of the notes. The whole thing went up."

The Professor heaved a sigh. "Now," he said, "we must destroy the rest of the machine."

"That's not going to be so easy," said Dan. "It's all metal and glass and wire mesh and stuff like that. Why don't we just hide it and say we've smashed it?"

"I suppose that would do as well."

Professor Bullfinch burrowed into the heaped-up junk and put the pieces of apparatus on the floor at the back of the bin. He piled other things over them until they were completely concealed.

"And now," he said, "let's go upstairs and find Colonel Twist. We must break the news to him that there is no longer any reason for him to guard the house."

12

The Professor Refuses

Colonel Twist took the news badly. He turned a curious shade of mildewy gray, and tottered feebly to a chair for support. Danny watched him with interest, wondering if he was going to faint. He had never seen anyone do so, and it was a matter of scientific curiosity to him.

"Do you mean to tell me," moaned the Colonel, "that you have broken up the machine and burned your notes?"

"I can smell the smoke," observed the Professor. "Luckily, the bench top is stone, so very little else will be damaged."

The Colonel pulled himself together and rushed to the lab. He shoved Corporal Blevitch aside, unlocked the door, and threw it open. A layer of smoke hung in the air. On the table could be seen a heap of delicate ash which fluttered away in the breeze from the opened door.

"Nothing," whimpered the Colonel. "Nothing left. I'll be court-martialed."

"It wasn't your fault," said the Professor soothingly. "You did everything you were told to."

"And there were no spies? Those—those children stole the machine? How—how—?"

"Sit down, please," said the Professor. "You look terrible. I'll tell you how it was done."

"I *feel* terrible," said the Colonel, sinking down on a stool.

The Professor told the whole story. When he had finished, he said, "You may as well send those other soldiers away. They'll do no more good here."

"I can't do that," Colonel Twist said. "I was ordered to guard the house and the laboratory, and I'll have to keep doing so until General Gruntle arrives."

"If you must, you must. I'm sorry for you," said the Professor. "As for me, I'm going to bed."

Dan followed him, with a last pitying glance at Colonel Twist.

Long past midnight, Danny was aroused by the sound of knocking at the front door. Awake in an instant, he hopped out of bed. He wouldn't have missed General Gruntle's arrival for anything. He didn't even wait to put on his slippers but hurried barefoot down the stairs. Colonel Twist, looking haggard and rumpled, was opening the door.

It was not General Gruntle who entered, however, but a tall, bony man with a long, sour face. Far from a glittering uniform covered with medals, he wore a sober black suit.

"Dr. Grimes!" Danny exclaimed.

"Good evening, Daniel," said Dr. Grimes, with a curt nod. And to the Colonel he said, "Colonel Twist? I am Dr. A. J. Grimes. Your soldiers outside tried to stop me. You have evidently carried out your orders. However, I have an order signed by the Chief of Staff requiring you to withdraw your men immediately and to leave this house."

He handed the Colonel a paper.

Colonel Twist read it. "To—to leave?" he said. "Right now?"

"That is correct."

Professor Bullfinch came down the stairs,

tying the cord of his bathrobe. "Hello, Grimes," he said. "These poor fellows haven't had any rest since heaven knows when. You needn't chase them out. Colonel, I'm sure Mrs. Dunn will put you up in the guest room, and your two soldiers can sleep on the living-room couch, which opens into a double bed. You can send the rest of the guards home. Come along into the kitchen, Grimes, and have some coffee. You look tired."

"I have flown direct from Washington," said Dr. Grimes. "Now that you mention it, I could do with a little refreshment."

A short time later, the Professor, Dr. Grimes, Mrs. Dunn, and Danny were all seated around the kitchen table. Mrs. Dunn had heated some blueberry muffins, and the Professor had made a pot of coffee.

"I was at the meeting when General Gruntle received the Colonel's phone call," Dr. Grimes explained, biting appreciatively into a muffin. "When I heard what was going on, I was furious, as you can imagine. I at once got in touch with the Chief of Staff and pointed out to him that if the news got out that a respected American scientist was being held prisoner in his own house and forced to give up his invention, it would cause an ex-

plosion bigger than that of a hydrogen bomb. Of course, he agreed. I knew perfectly well that no foreign spies had heard of the machine or stolen it. I know you, Bullfinch, and I was certain you had found a way of removing it from its guards. I was right, wasn't I?"

"Yes. With the help of Dan and his friends, I recovered it. I'm afraid we gave poor Colonel Twist a hard time."

"Well, that's all over with, now. Will you show it to me?"

"I'm afraid that's impossible," said the Professor. "It has been destroyed, and all my notes as well."

"What?" Dr. Grimes looked very grim. "I always knew you were a feather-brained dreamer, Bullfinch, but this is utterly foolish. What made you do such a thing?"

The Professor stirred his coffee pensively. Then, putting down the spoon with a decisive click, he said, "I decided that the time was not yet quite ripe for such an invention. It would be like giving a child a loaded pistol to play with."

"I know you must feel that way because of the experience you've been subjected to," said Dr. Grimes. "But you see how quickly I set it right. It's not as bad as you think."

The Professor looked sharply at Dr. Grimes. "Can you guarantee me," he said, "that the invisibility simulator will *not* fall into the wrong hands?"

Dr. Grimes tried to meet the Professor's gaze, and failed. "Perhaps not," he said. "But all that is needed are the proper safeguards. Look here, Bullfinch, you know perfectly well that a scientific advance cannot be suppressed. At this very moment, someone else may be developing the same thing. To destroy it—"

"Oh, it still exists." The Professor smiled. He tapped his forehead. "It's in here. All I'm asking for, from you, is a little patience."

"Patience?"

"Certainly. We tend to jump into things without thinking—a bit like my dear friend Danny, here. Don't blush, Dan. There's plenty of excuse for you. But there's not much excuse, for instance, for people who build atomic reactor plants before they have worked out the problems of waste disposal for radioactive materials. We used DDT for years without first carefully studying its effects on our ecology, and found out its dangers almost too late. We have hurried into all sorts of technological improvements and then found later that we were poisoning our water supply. All I'm asking for, Grimes, is a breathing space for the invisibility simulator until we determine how to control the invention and *who* is to control it."

Dr. Grimes sat back in his chair. He looked as if he had bitten into a lemon.

"And that's your last word, is it?" he said.

"Not quite."

The Professor reached out and put an arm around Danny's shoulders.

"It may take some time for us to learn how to handle all the power of new inventions," he said. "Here's the future, Grimes. Let's give it a chance."

Slowly, Dr. Grimes's expression softened.

His leathery cheeks creased in an unexpected smile.

"Ah, well," he said, reaching for the plate, "it was worth coming all the way from Washington for some of these blueberry muffins."

ABOUT THE AUTHORS
AND ILLUSTRATOR

JAY WILLIAMS has written over twenty-five fiction and non-fiction books for children of all ages, in addition to coauthoring fifteen books about Danny Dunn. Mr. Williams was born in Buffalo, New York, and educated at the University of Pennsylvania, Columbia University, and the Art Students League.

RAYMOND ABRASHKIN wrote and coproduced the very popular and successful "Little Fugitive," a film that won an award at the Venice Film Festival.

PAUL SAGSOORIAN was born in New York and studied art at several art schools in New York City. A freelancer, he works for art studios, advertising agencies, and book publishers.

29990 THE GREATEST MONSTERS IN THE WORLD, by Daniel Cohen. Illustrated with reproductions and photographs. The intriguing pros and cons of the existence of Bigfoot, Nessie, the Yeti, and many other possible and impossible monsters. ($1.50)

29802 SEA MONSTERS, written and illustrated by Walter Buehr. A fascinating discussion of the myths, facts, and scientific theories about the existence of giant sea creatures from prehistoric times to the present. ($1.25)

29953 GREAT MONSTERS OF THE MOVIES, by Edward Edelson. Illustrated with stills from the films. This survey of one of the most popular scary entertainments in this century covers the legends behind the stories and the brilliant directors and actors who created some of the most successful horror films. ($1.50)

29749 GREAT SCIENCE FICTION FROM THE MOVIES, by Edward Edelson. Illustrated with stills. This entertaining history reveals the intriguing combination of scientific fact and writers' imagination that has produced some of the most thought-provoking, strange, and exciting films of the twentieth century. ($1.25)

29797 THE SECRET OF GRANDFATHER'S DIARY, by Milton Lomask. Illustrated by W. T. Mars. At his Grandmother's house, Denny solves a strange and baffling mystery involving an unknown thief who steals nothing but seemingly worthless old toys. ($1.25)

29817 FOG MAGIC, by Julia L. Sauer. Illustrated by Lynd Ward. When Greta walks through the fog, she starts off on an adventure that takes her back to the past of one hundred years ago. ($1.25)

29948 BASIL OF BAKER STREET, by Eve Titus. Illustrated by Paul Galdone. The Mystery of the Missing Twins was one of the strangest and most baffling cases in the famous career of Basil— Sherlock Holmes of the mouse world. ($1.50)

29866 BASIL AND THE PYGMY CATS, by Eve Titus. Illustrated by Paul Galdone. Follow Basil to the mysterious East in one of the most perplexing cases of his famed career as the Sherlock Holmes of the mouse community. ($1.25)

29984